Audra

Delaney Diamond

Garden Avenue Press

Audra by Delaney Diamond

Prologue

"What did you think of my speech?" Damon asked.

He and Audra entered the house from the garage and stepped into the kitchen. Tonight, he accepted an award as the year's Sports Humanitarian for his charitable donations and the time he spent mentoring and coaching young boys.

"Like I told you weeks ago, it was good," she said, making her way to the foyer.

He followed her up the stairs. The house was quiet because their three children weren't there. They hadn't been sure what time they would get home, so the kids spent the night at her mother's before they went to the event.

"Good as in okay, or good as in I killed it?" Damon asked.

He always practiced his speeches in front of Audra, and she gave him pointers, not only for the delivery but for the speech itself. He trusted her writing skills, and when she gave a suggestion, he made the revisions. But practice in the den was a whole different animal than delivering in front of a room filled with people hanging on his every word.

"You killed it," Audra said.

They entered the master bedroom at the end of the hall.

"You're right, I killed it."

Audra flipped on the light and illuminated their bedroom.

She slanted a glance over her shoulder. Her hair swished with the movement, bone straight and shimmering black from a silk press. "Careful, your head is growing," she teased.

He laughed, watching as she stepped out of her heels with fluid movements. Feminine and casually graceful. His wife was so sexy.

"You said I did good," he reminded her.

"Mhmm. Actually, you did fantastic, hon. I have to give you some sugar for that."

With the shoes dangling from her fingers, she stood on tiptoe and kissed his bearded cheek, her lips soft as rose petals. The blood leaped under his skin. They hadn't had sex in a while, but maybe he'd get lucky tonight.

He shrugged off his jacket and tossed it onto one of the chairs in front of the fireplace.

Like the rest of the house, Audra had handled the decor. The master bedroom was designed with an eye for comfort and simple elegance, with a California king bed and a custom-built tufted headboard reaching almost to the high ceiling. With no television in the room, the focal point was the fireplace surrounded by polished alabaster tiles, above which hung an abstract painting from an up-and-coming local artist. Teal armchairs and a cocktail table rested in front of the fireplace. Throw pillows and drapes in cool colors like green and blue contrasted against the white and tan in the bedsheets and on the walls.

"I'm very proud of you." Audra went into her large walk-in closet.

Damon went to stand in the doorway, his mouth watering as she slipped the black dress down her arms and stepped out of it, revealing skin the color of deepest, darkest brown sugar and the luscious curves of her hourglass figure. She wore a black lace bra and matching thong, which disappeared between her ample butt cheeks.

"As long as you think I did well, that's all that matters," he said. "By the way, I forgot to tell you that Simon texted me during the program. TAG Heuer contacted him. They want to re-up my contract."

Ever since he quit playing baseball, Damon expanded his income through modeling, licensing deals, and investments. The flexibility of being able to set his own schedule and not having to answer to anyone gave him more time to spend with his family. His friend and attorney, Simon Finch, negotiated the modeling and licensing deals.

"Are you interested?" Audra hung up her dress and started removing her bra and jewelry.

His body stirred with desire as he watched her disrobe, an erection straining the front of his pants. "Definitely. I like the watches, so they're an easy sell."

He promoted the TAG Heuer sports collection, and a drawer in his closet was filled with their watches. At the moment, he wore the Carrera Porsche Chronograph Special Edition timepiece—the most expensive one in the line.

"I'm guessing you told Simon yes?" Audra slipped on a cute white pajama set, made up of shorts and a top with thin straps.

"I did," Damon answered.

She came toward him, a smile reflected in her pretty dark eyes, her round face accentuated by sinfully full lips.

When she exited the closet, he gently tugged her close. Slipping an arm around her waist, he kissed her on the mouth.

He had only meant to be affectionate, but she smelled good, wearing a rose and orange blossom perfume. The combination of that scent and her soft body inflamed his desire. But as he deepened the kiss, she tensed in his arms and pulled back, placing a hand on his chest.

"Honey, I need to wash off my makeup."

"Wash it off later. I'm trying to get a little something, something," he said with a wicked grin. One hand coasted low and grabbed her ass.

Audra became more tense and edged away from his hand, her face apologetic. "Not tonight. It's been a long day, and I'm tired. I'm not in the mood."

Heat flamed Damon's neck, and he reluctantly released her. "Seems you're hardly ever in the mood nowadays," he remarked, keeping his voice neutral.

He didn't want to start a fight, but she pulled away from him more often than not lately.

"That's not true. We had sex a couple weeks ago," Audra said.

"A month ago," Damon corrected.

Her eyebrows drew together. "Has it been that long?"

"Yeah."

She dodged his eyes and veered toward the bathroom. "Oh," she said in a low voice.

Damon didn't respond, instead going to his own walk-in closet and removing his clothes with frustrated yanks. He changed into pajama bottoms, then returned to the bedroom where he removed the throw pillows from the bed and placed them on a shelf of the armoire, below the extra pillows, blankets, and sheets. He paused, eyes resting on the locked box on the bottom shelf that contained "toys" for when they were feeling a little kinky. It contained a couple of vibrators, Ben Wa balls, a vinyl whip, nipple clamps, lubricant, fur-lined hand-cuffs, and a mask. He couldn't remember the last time they had unlocked the box and used any of the contents.

After he turned off the light, he slipped under the thin blanket and lay supine on the mattress with his arms folded behind his head and his penis at half-mast.

Audra used to enjoy his touch. Hell, she used to initiate sex. He never dreamed he'd see the day when she talked about sex as if once every two weeks was sufficient. Desire burned through him at the slightest brush of her body against his, but if he was being brutally honest, she behaved as if she no longer wanted him to touch her at all, and his ego was taking a beating.

She exited the bathroom, and in the ambient light, he saw her rubbing lotion on her hands and elbows. His eyes followed her until she slipped under the covers with him.

"Maybe we can do something tomorrow night," she said.

The words chafed.

Pity sex.

"Nah, I'm good. If you don't want to, you don't have to," Damon said, staring up into the darkness.

"It's not that I don't want to," Audra said in a small voice.

Coulda fooled me, he thought.

"Are you upset?" she asked.

"No."

"Talk to me."

"About what?"

"Tell me what you're thinking."

He smothered a sigh. She always complained that he didn't talk enough. He knew that but couldn't bring himself to open up more.

"You don't want to know what I'm thinking, Audra."

"I do."

"No, you don't." He rolled onto his side, away from her. "Good night."

"Damon—"

"Good night, Audra."

Quiet filled the room for a while.

"Good night," she finally whispered.

Chapter One

Six months later

"Kids, come on! You're going to be late!" Audra yelled the words through the French doors leading from the kitchen into the foyer.

Shaking her head and muttering to herself, she placed breakfast plates on the table by the bay window but turned at the sound of movement behind her.

Her eldest, fifteen-year-old Kerilyn, sauntered into the kitchen with a backpack over one shoulder and her head bent toward the phone in her hand. Golden-skinned, she wore clothes that signified what Audra dubbed her "black phase." Lately, most of her outfits consisted of all black. Today, black jeans and a black blouse with silver necklaces dangling around her neck and silver earrings in her ears. Her dark hair, parted in the middle, hung in silky sheets that framed her face.

"Where's your brother and sister?"

"On their way." Kerilyn finally lifted her gaze from the phone. "Hey, Mom. Can I ask you something?"

Audra stifled a sigh. It was never a good sign when one of her offspring wanted to ask her something.

"Go ahead." She placed a glass pitcher of orange juice on the table.

"Don't freak out, but... can I get a tattoo?"

This child...

Audra locked eyes with her daughter. "No."

"Just like that? No?"

Audra took glasses from the cabinet and placed them on the table. "You asked, I answered."

"That's so unfair," Kerilyn whined.

"How is that unfair?"

"You never let me do anything."

"Keri, you're fifteen."

"But I'm almost sixteen. What's wrong with me getting a tattoo? Brenda's mother let her get a rose tattoo on her ankle. I don't want a big one. Just a little butterfly on my ankle."

"The answer is no."

"Why not?"

"A tattoo is permanent."

"Dad has a bunch of tattoos."

Audra placed two platters with breakfast on the table. Today she tried something new—almond butter on toast, topped with fruit.

"Your father was an adult when he got his. I told you before, after you turn eighteen, you can do whatever you want."

Most of Damon's tats were baseball related, and there was some scripture on his chest.

"Why does everything hinge on me being eighteen?"

"Because at eighteen, you're legally an adult, Keri, and I hope by then you'll be able to make good decisions. For now, the answer is no."

Kerilyn pouted. "It's my body."

Audra arched an eyebrow. "Your body is under my roof, and as long as your body is under my roof, you're not getting a tattoo."

"But—"

"*Enough.* This conversation is over. Sit down for breakfast."

Kerilyn dropped her book bag to the floor beside her chair with a loud thump and muttered under her breath.

Audra glared at her. "What was that?"

Kerilyn glanced over her shoulder. "Nothing," she said in a quiet voice.

"That's what I thought."

Audra left the kitchen and stood at the foot of the staircase, hands on her hips. "Tracy! Junior! I need to see your faces right now."

Each morning, she woke them up after much nudging, cajoling, and threats of taking away their electronics. They went to school five days a week yet acted surprised and miserable every morning. After making sure they went into the bathroom, brushed their teeth, and washed their faces, she left them alone to get dressed, so she could make breakfast before they went to school.

Once again, not new information, yet every morning she had to yell for them to come downstairs.

"Coming, Mommy!" Junior yelled.

She heard scampering feet and giggles. Her two youngest appeared at the top of the staircase, dragging their book bags with them. Seven-year-old Tracy with twists capped by pink, white, and clear beads, and eight-year-old Damon Junior with a low-cut fade.

"Chop, chop," Audra said, clapping her hands. She assessed their attire, making sure they wore socks, were fully dressed in jeans and shirts, and neither wore mismatched tennis shoes, which had occurred an alarming number of times.

They dropped their bags at the bottom of the stairs and raced ahead of her into the kitchen. They seemed to always be racing, running, and jumping. Once settled across from each other—Junior in a chair and Tracy on the bench—Junior picked up a piece of toast and started eating right away.

"What's this?" Tracy, the picky eater, wrinkled her nose at the food.

"Something new. Try it." Audra poured orange juice into their glasses.

"Mom's testing one of the ideas from her blog," Kerilyn said, her voice containing a hint of sarcasm.

When Audra shot a glance at her, her face showed nothing but innocence.

Tracy placed a piece of toast on her plate and then sniffed the open face sandwich. She crossed her arms. "I don't want it. Can I have cereal?"

"We're out of milk," Audra lied.

Tracy was getting to the point where only air satisfied her. She didn't like her food to touch and resisted trying anything new. In no mood to accommodate her daughter's finicky eating this morning, Audra turned away from the table and went back to the island to clean up.

Damon strolled into the kitchen. "Morning," he said, his voice a low rumble. The spicy scent of his aftershave filled the air as he walked by.

"Good morning," Kerilyn, Junior, and Tracy chorused.

"Good morning," Audra added, as heat alighted under her skin.

Her gaze skipped to his wide back and unhurried stride. A former professional baseball player who retired several years ago, he moved with lithe, graceful steps.

With the T-shirt hanging over his distressed jeans, she couldn't see his butt but knew the jeans fit snug on his firm bottom the same way the cotton top clung to his chest and broad shoulders. Diamond studs glinted in each earlobe. Including a square, bearded jawline and piercing brown eyes, he reeked of virility and sex appeal.

"There's more to life than baseball," he said in an interview after announcing his retirement.

The sporting world had been shocked and disappointed by his decision. Only thirty-three at the time, they expected at least a few more good playing years from him. Instead, he left at the height of his career and focused his attention on his family and expanding his business portfolio.

Damon sat at the head of the table, across from Kerilyn.

"Daddy, I don't want this," Tracy whined.

"What's wrong with it?" Damon asked.

Audra snapped the covers on the containers of berries and placed the butter knife in the sink.

"I don't like it," Tracy answered.

"She hasn't even tasted it." Junior licked almond butter from the corner of his mouth. "Try it, it's good."

Damon bit off a piece of toast and chewed. "Mmm. Junior's right. Tastes fine to me."

Tracy slouched on the bench and hung her head, essentially digging in her heels.

"Can I have her breakfast?" Junior asked.

"No, you can't," Damon said.

"Aww," Junior said, disappointed.

"Tracy, you have to eat something. You can't go to school with an empty stomach." Audra swept crumbs onto her palm and tossed them in the trash.

"You want some honey on your bread?" Damon asked.

"Okay," Tracy said in a low, miserable voice.

He lifted the honey from the middle of the table and drizzled the sweetener on his daughter's toast. "Try it now."

11

Watching from nearby, Audra popped a blueberry in her mouth.

Tracy took a tiny, suspicious bite.

"How is it?" Damon asked.

"Good." Her little feet swung under the table. A positive sign. Crisis averted.

While they ate—laughing and talking at the table—Audra went into the den, which opened from the kitchen with a vaulted ceiling and comfortable chairs arranged to maximize television watching. Using the computer in the corner, she logged into the school's system to check the calendar for the upcoming week because she had failed to do that over the weekend. She responded to a question from one of the teachers and then started her to-do list for the day. By the time she reached the end and returned to the kitchen, her family had finished breakfast and were on their feet.

One by one, they placed their dishes in the sink.

"Dad, can I drive today?" Kerilyn asked.

"Yeah, you can drive." Damon tossed her the keys.

She caught them. "Yes!" She rushed out of the kitchen first.

"Bye," Audra called after her.

Her daughter grunted an answer. Audra longed for a better relationship between them. She wanted the type of relationship she had with her mother—cooking together, going shopping, and on spa dates. No such luck with her daughter. Kerilyn saw her as an annoyance.

"Bye-bye, Mommy." Tracy rushed over and Audra bent to kiss both her cheeks. Unlike her big sister, she could be very affectionate. After the kiss, she scampered off.

"Bye, Mommy." Junior ran out the door after his sisters.

"Bye, baby."

Damon paused on his way out the door. "I have a business

meeting this afternoon. Could you pick up the kids from school?"

"Sure, that won't be a problem," Audra said.

"Might be home late, so... you know."

"Don't hold dinner for you." As usual. She forced a smile and hoped it appeared natural.

"Right."

There was always something. A meeting, an event, hanging with the fellas, or some vague excuse when he ran out of lies. She didn't know why he bothered giving a reason anymore. She'd become used to his absence.

"What about Friday? Are you coming to Bruno's to see the renovations? I need to tell him, so he'll have an accurate head-count for the food."

Her stepbrother, Bruno, had invited the whole family to take a look at his kitchen and outdoor dining renovations. She already guessed Damon wouldn't be going, and Bruno would cook plenty of food regardless, to accommodate their large, blended family.

"That's this Friday? I'm not gonna be able to go. I'll have to see the changes he made another time."

An absolutely unsurprising answer.

"Okay."

"I'll see you later." Damon headed out the door.

No hug, no kiss goodbye. The first years of their marriage had been a feast of touches, winks, ass-grabs, and kisses. The last six months or so had been a dearth of affection.

From the island, Audra could see straight into the tiled foyer with a good view of the front door. The children had already gone to the car. Damon picked up the duffel bag he left near the door before coming in for breakfast.

She waited to see if he'd turn once. Glance in her direction.

Acknowledge her one last time before finally leaving. He didn't. He closed the door, and silence enveloped the house.

In zombie-like slow motion, Audra wiped down the table. Tracy had left her plate with half the toast eaten after picking the blueberries and sliced strawberries off the top. She finished her daughter's portion and rinsed the plates before stacking them in the dishwasher with the glasses, all the while Damon's cool attitude replaying in her mind.

A wave of pain undulated through her, and she gripped the edge of the sink and closed her eyes, determined not to cry. This happened every so often. She hadn't gotten used to the sting of his indifference—a man who at one time claimed he'd rather spend time with her than hang with the boys.

She refused to cry. Not today. She had a million tasks to complete.

She took a deep, quivering breath, wishing she knew how to fix their broken marriage but afraid to reach out. Afraid to ask the tough questions and dig deeper into Damon's whereabouts at night. Her husband was a highly sexual man, and her mind veered away from the obvious. Very likely, another woman.

That would explain why he no longer attended family functions and some nights came home at a god-awful hour. That would explain why he hadn't touched her in six long months.

If he wasn't getting it at home, he was getting it elsewhere. Wasn't that the saying?

Chapter Two

Damon exited the locker room at Fit Body Gyms in black shorts and a blue tank top and went in search of his buddies. He found them at the weights.

Simon Finch was blond-haired, blue-eyed, and almost ten years older. Damon knew him from when he lived in Minnesota and played professional ball for the Twins. They lost contact when Damon moved to Atlanta but ran into each other one day. Turned out, Simon had also moved to Atlanta and worked for a law practice in Buckhead.

Tall and thin, everything about him was long. Long arms. Long legs. Long face. When he told Damon he was leaving his firm to set up his own practice, Damon introduced him to friends who could use his services.

The newer member of their friendship circle, and the man spotting Simon at the weights, was Zack Stolz. Half Black, half Chinese, the former pitcher was five years older than Damon. They'd met him at the juice bar downstairs and struck up a friendship.

Damon nodded as he approached. "Hey, what's up."

"You're late. Glad you could join us," Zack remarked sarcastically.

Damon snorted. Zack had a smart mouth.

"Junior's principal needed to talk to me when I dropped the kids off at school. Seems he's getting a bit mouthy with his social studies teacher by challenging her in front of the class."

"Isn't that why you send them to that expensive private school? So they can be independent thinkers?" Zack asked.

"Yeah, but apparently, he's cutting up for laughs. I swear that kid thinks he's a standup comedian sometimes."

He got that trait from his mother. Audra was always cracking lame jokes. At least, she used to.

Simon looked up at him from the bench. "Kids will keep you on your toes, won't they?"

"Tell me about it," Damon muttered.

They spent the next hour and a half doing weights and cardio. After the intense workout, they completed cool-down exercises and then walked downstairs to the gym's juice bar. Damon didn't miss the looks they received, either from people who knew him and Zack as former athletes, or because they were simply checking out three attractive men. That wasn't vanity talking. He turned heads from way back when he played ball and became known as Damon "The Flash" Foster.

He and his friends sat at one of the tables in the corner with their juice orders.

"So, did you buy the car?" Zack asked Simon.

With a wide grin, Simon pulled out his phone and showed them the lemon-yellow Lamborghini he purchased over the weekend.

Damon whistled. "That's nice. Fully loaded?"

"All the bells and whistles. Best birthday present I ever bought myself." Simon couldn't stop smiling as he gazed at the photo.

"I can't believe Elsa let you buy that midlife crisis car." Zack shook his head.

"It's not a car. It's an experience."

"Yeah, yeah, whatever."

"Don't try to steal my joy because Claire won't let you do shit."

"Who you talking to? I'm an alpha male. I run my house." Zack pounded his chest.

Laughing, Damon shook his head and sipped on his carrot-ginger-turmeric combination. "Pretty sure if you have to tell people you're an alpha male, chances are you're not an alpha male."

He and Simon bumped fists.

"He's got you there," Simon says.

"I'm not paying him any mind," Zack said. "He stays at the office all night to avoid going home."

The humor leaked out of Damon. "I have a lot of work to do."

"Bull. Shit."

Simon eyed him with genuine concern. "Is everything okay with you and Audra?"

Damon rubbed the back of his neck. "We all right."

Zack frowned. "Hey man, I was kidding, but is there a problem? Come on, you're among friends."

Damon groaned inwardly. Sharing his feelings was diffi-cult. The first half of his childhood, he'd grown up in a house-hold where closed fists demanded silence, so he learned to be quiet during tense or emotional moments. He used to joke that the punches toughened him up, but the bruises went deeper than surface level and turned him into a scared, insecure youth with little to no self-esteem. Baseball and the love and patience of his adoptive parents had changed his life and healed the gaping wounds from the days he lived in torment.

"We're going through some shit, that's all," he replied.

Zack groaned. "Come on, you two are the blueprint. Whenever me and my wife argue, I think about you guys and how great your relationship is."

Simon nodded in agreement.

"You don't want what we have now," Damon muttered.

What he and Audra presented to the world was not their reality. He'd seen the photos of them captioned with #RelationshipGoals. The blended family of five, with the former athlete and the stylish homemaker. From the outside, they looked happy, but behind the scenes was not nearly as attractive.

"Is it really that bad?" Simon asked.

The tone of their conversation had changed.

"Have either of you brought up the D word?" Zack asked.

Divorce. Pain lanced through his chest. "Nah. I'm not worried about that," Damon said.

Liar. Divorce loomed on the horizon. He knew it, felt it. The promise echoed in his bones the same way his father's arthritic knees portended rain.

"Whew, that's good at least. That means you can work through whatever is wrong until she calls it quits. You ever noticed it's always women who initiate divorce? When was the last time you heard of a man asking for a divorce?" Zack asked.

"They don't have to put up with our shit anymore, that's why, and they're not afraid to be alone," Simon said.

"Shoulda never let them work," Zack mumbled.

Simon and Damon swung their heads in his direction.

"I'm kidding!" Zack said with a laugh. "You have a good woman in Audra, and I'm sure your relationship will improve. Has she stopped giving you sex yet? That's the number one thing they go to."

Not totally comfortable with the direction of the conversation, Damon shifted in his chair. He and Audra rarely slept in the same bed anymore. "Things have slowed between us."

Zack nodded his head at the confirmation and lowered his voice. "Sometimes you have to shake things up, man. Have you considered an open marriage?"

Simon stared at Zack with incredulity. "How the hell would that help?"

Damon laughed in shock. "You have got to be kidding."

"Don't knock it till you try it." Zack sipped his green juice.

"You're serious," Damon said.

"Sure am."

Damon's eyes narrowed. "Are you saying what I think you're saying? You and Claire...?"

Zack nodded with a smug expression.

Simon laughed. "You sneaky bastard."

"And opening your marriage worked?" Damon asked in disbelief.

"Sure did, when we went through a rough patch five years ago. All that crazy, out-of-control stuff you see on TV and in the movies is bull shit. Having other partners can really spice up your sex life. It saved our marriage." Zack spoke in a matter-of-fact way.

"Look, I'm not judging, but no way in hell I'm giving my wife permission to fuck another man," Damon said.

"Maybe she already has," Zack said with a slick smile. "You have an attractive wife. Somebody might have already slipped through the back door. *You're* not fucking her."

Damon glared at him, body vibrating with the energy needed to refrain from leaping over the table and putting a fist through his friend's face for speaking his worst nightmare aloud. He couldn't imagine a fate worse than losing Audra to another man. The very idea was enough to make him lose his mind.

"Dammit, Zack, what's wrong with you? That's his wife you're talking about," Simon said.

"I'm just saying it happens, and taking on other partners is a viable option. Claire and I are good now, but I'm not opposed to doing it again." Zack shrugged.

"That's not something I want to try." Damon leaned across the table and locked eyes with the other man. "And do us both a favor. Don't talk about my wife again."

Zack threw up his hands in a disarming way. "Okay, fine, forget Audra. What about you? She's cut you off, and you have needs, don't you?"

Damon resettled in the chair. "I'm not risking a divorce."

"Be discreet."

"Are you listening to yourself?" Simon turned to Damon. "Don't cheat on your wife."

"You don't have to tell me. I almost lost Audra once before."

"When?" Zack asked.

"Way back, man, before we got married. I didn't do shit, but she cut me off. Longest six weeks of my life. I'm not risking that again." That's how he'd known she was *the one*.

"Okay, bruh, you have to tell us the story. What happened?"

As a professional athlete, Damon damn near had his pick of women in any city in the country. Truth be told, he'd been a hoe, certain he would never find love and not bothering to look for the elusive emotion. He'd enjoyed the parties and women until Audra walked into a party at his condo. Cliché as it sounded, she wasn't like the other women. Didn't even know who he was. Meeting her changed everything.

Cute in a pair of shorts and a sleeveless top, she didn't seem to be trying hard at all, which made her stand out. She was so... normal. He immediately started hitting on her.

She didn't give him a chance, though, which made him

work that much harder. Over several weeks, he bombarded her with flowers and gifts. He popped up unannounced at her job a couple of times, at the end of the work day. Looking back, that was some stalker behavior, and he was lucky she didn't call the cops on him.

When she *finally* agreed to go out with him, he felt as if he'd won the World Series. They moved slowly, and she didn't sleep with him for months. Once they slept together, he assumed he had her in the bag. Wrong.

"I went on a fake date with a Victoria Secret model. Her manager arranged for us to attend a party together for publicity. I didn't even sleep with the woman, but Audra saw the pictures online, and we had a huge fight about it."

His explanation to her fell on deaf ears. With one hand propped on her hip and the other jabbing dangerously close to his face, she declared, "I will not, I mean absolutely *not* turn a blind eye to your indiscretions. If you want to hoe around while in a committed relationship, look elsewhere." His sweet-natured girlfriend had turned into a hellcat.

She stopped speaking to him. Cut him off for *forty-two* days. The longest month and a half of his life. He had been stressed that he would never win her over. When he finally convinced her to give them another chance, he promised himself he wouldn't risk losing her again.

Now they were in this strange limbo of a marriage. Barely speaking and dancing around each other, afraid to say the wrong thing and cause an explosion.

"At least you learned your lesson," Zack said.

Suddenly weary and disgruntled, Damon didn't want to discuss his marital woes anymore. "I gotta run. I'll see you guys later, all right?" His chair scraped along the cement floor as he stood with an abrupt motion.

His friends raised their eyebrows in surprise.

"Okay man, we'll catch up later," Zack said.

"See you later," Simon said.

Damon returned to the locker room to get his bag and clothes. He'd take a shower at the office.

He climbed into his old-gold Range Rover but didn't drive off right away. He went to Audra's Instagram page. At the advice of her younger sister, Monica—a social media influencer —she set up a profile. She'd become an influencer in her own right with a small following of over 80,000 people.

Staring at her face in one photo, his chest tightened. She wore a coy smile, flirting with the camera. His forefinger traced the side of her face. They hardly touched anymore. Some days, he stayed away from home, so he wouldn't have to fight the constant animalistic urge to ravish his own wife.

He scrolled through her posts. Most were photos and videos of the items she promoted on her Mommy lifestyle blog, Plush, which started as a hobby but had taken on a life of its own. She made a little money from affiliate links and endorse- ments. A photo of her with her eyes closed caught his attention. She wore a pleased smile on her face as she inhaled the aroma of a large pink candle. He recognized it as one of many she kept in their bedroom.

There were also personal and family-focused images, including one of him and her reclining on chairs on the beach while they vacationed at their property in the Dominican Republic. A Dominican teammate had told him about the reasonable prices of property there and hooked him up with a bilingual agent in the country.

His eyes lingered on a black-and-white of Audra at the same beach—only a headshot—shielding her eyes from the sun. Then he paused on a short video of her mixing batter while Tracy peered in the bowl from her position on a stool in the kitchen.

For Throwback Thursday, she shared a birthday picture of herself holding a bunch of balloons in a pastel mini-dress that hugged every luscious curve of her body. She turned thirty that year. He paused at another Throwback Thursday photo of her and the kids from about three years ago. She sat on a chair with Tracy on her lap and Junior and Kerilyn on either side of her.

He smiled briefly. His family. They looked so happy.

He skimmed the comments of some of the posts. Most of her followers were women, but a few males were present and had a habit of making inappropriate comments.

Ur beautiful. Thicc like I like my women.

Damon saw red. He shook off the flash of anger and clicked on the profile. Some big-necked wanna-be trainer right here in Atlanta.

Marry me, a dickhead in DC wrote.

Been looking my whole life for a woman like you. Atlanta again.

Didn't these assholes see she had a husband and family? They couldn't see the big ass ring on her finger? Normally, he wouldn't care, but with his marriage on the rocks, and Zack's words rewinding in his head, their flirtatious words inflamed his jealousy.

You're not fucking her.

If Audra wanted to cheat, she had plenty of options.

Chapter Three

Audra removed a bunch of advertisements and offers from the mailbox at the end of the drive. One of the neighbors honked as he sped by with his dog hanging out the window, and she waved.

The swim and tennis community of Lakeland Crossing contained all brick, custom-built homes. Their house was located on a prime lot with the backyard butting up to the lake. This plot of land had been the last lakeside lot available and resulted in a bidding war. Lucky for her, Damon had deeper pockets than the other family and was doubly deter-mined to purchase the parcel because she had said she wanted it.

"Anything you want," he used to say.

True enough, over the years, he'd spoiled her.

The widower two doors down approached in tennis shoes and a tracksuit. Every afternoon, he took a walk around the neighborhood. Gray hairs and fine lines carved into his brown face didn't detract from his handsome features. She had never met his wife because he moved in a couple years after she passed, but he always spoke about her with fondness in his voice.

"Hello, Audra."

"Hi, Bob."

"I finally sold the company," he said.

"That's great news. Congratulations!"

He owned—used to own—a software company with a lucrative government contract.

"I have a lot of free time now."

"Isn't that what we all long for?"

Humor filled his eyes. "True. I wish my Delores was here. Retirement would be much sweeter."

Audra hummed her sympathy because she couldn't think of anything adequate to say. Telling him he'd find someone else seemed inappropriate, especially when he held his dead wife in such high regard. A couple of times she considered introducing him to her mother, but Bob didn't seem ready to move on yet.

"I'll see you later," he said.

"Have a good afternoon."

Audra entered the house and crossed the tiled floor into the kitchen to the right. Dinner simmered on the stove, perfuming the air with the smell of Cajun style chicken in a creamy tomato sauce. She only needed to add fresh pasta to the boiling water in the other pot. The simple dinner was filled with flavor, but she had prepared a separate meal of chicken fingers and sweet potato fries for her finicky eater, Tracy.

She dropped the mail on the countertop and cast a glance out the bay window at the large backyard enclosed by a privacy fence. Damon was playing baseball with Kerilyn, Junior, and Tracy. If they went out the gate, they'd be very close to the water's edge and the path that circled the lake.

The carpet of verdant grass held an adjustable basketball hoop for children, a trampoline, and a backyard playground set.

Two summers ago, Damon built a treehouse, and he'd also put together a she shed so Audra could have an office.

Some afternoons, he took their kids for a bike ride around the lake, a trail of four with Kerilyn in front and Damon pulling up the rear to keep an eye on the little ones.

The backyard was a haven of basketball games, frisbee throws, tag, and water balloon fights. Some days she'd call them for dinner, and Damon and the two youngest would keep playing until she threatened to toss the food in the trash.

When they came rushing in, Damon would give her a sweaty kiss, and she'd chase the children into the half bathroom to wash up for dinner. Kerilyn might saunter downstairs if she hadn't been outside with them.

Audra's eyes idled on her husband, his skin rich, as if milk chocolate had been molded over the bones of his face. One of the most handsome men she had ever laid eyes on.

She lowered her gaze to his thighs in gray shorts, thick and muscular and putting tree trunks to shame. His exposed arms were filled with tattoos of baseball, the numbers from the two teams he played on, and other images. He had such a beautiful physique, but lovely as his arms and thighs were, they weren't her favorite part of his anatomy.

She adored his back most of all and could write songs about the beauty of the quilt of muscles that traversed from his shoulders to right above his butt. She absolutely loved resting her head on him with an arm curled around his waist while they laid in bed together.

Bent over Tracy, he helped her hold the plastic bat. When Kerilyn pitched the plastic ball, Damon helped Tracy swing, and Audra heard a soft pop when the bat connected.

"Run! Run!" Junior screamed, jumping up and down.

Audra covered her mouth and laughed as Tracy rounded the bases, her little legs going fast, her face scrunched up in deep concentration as her long twists bounced behind her. Kerilyn pretended to struggle to retrieve the ball, and Tracy sailed home with a wide grin on her face. Damon pulled her into a celebratory lift while they all screamed as if she'd hit a home run in the last inning of a tie game.

Audra's heart swelled with happiness. Damon's bond with their children was unmistakable.

He was determined not to be the kind of father he had as a child. His father had been a monster—a loud drunk who struck fear in the hearts of his small family. The kids adored Damon, including Kerilyn, though she wasn't his biological daughter. He always referred to her as his and treated her the same as the other two. He had been the father figure she needed right from the beginning.

Kerilyn's father was a musician, Audra's first love and the man she lost her virginity to. He checked in twice a year for Christmas and Kerilyn's birthday, but otherwise, they didn't hear from him. The consummate bachelor, he traveled the world as the drummer in an Afropunk band. To prove what a great father he was, he never failed to show off the gifts he sent to Kerilyn on his social media handles. Expensive, extravagant gifts for Christmas and her birthday when all she really wanted was his time.

The phone rang, grabbing Audra's attention from the scene outside.

"Hi, Dena," she greeted Damon's adoptive mother.

Years ago, he retired her, but before that, she had spent almost two decades as a social worker within a very broken system in Arkansas. Damon had been removed from an abusive home where his father beat him and his mother whenever the alcoholic urge hit, and for Dena, he became more than a case file. She convinced her husband they should foster him. A year later, when Damon's mother and father signed away their parental rights, they adopted him at eleven years old.

"Hi. I tried that new cream you recommended, and I *love* how it has transformed my skin."

As research for her blog, Audra often found great products for reasonable prices and shared them with family and friends.

With the phone wedged between her ear and shoulder, she lowered the linguine into the pot. "I told you."

"I've been using it for a month now, and my skin is more supple and glowing. Chad says I'm aging backwards." Dena laughed.

They continued to chat, catching up because they hadn't talked in a while. Audra updated her on how the kids were doing in school, including the awards ceremony for Kerilyn the following evening, and how she regularly drove Audra crazy by pushing back against her authority.

"I don't envy you," Dena said with feeling.

"I don't want her to make the same mistakes I did. I went through a period where I drove Mom and Benicio crazy, giving into peer pressure and doing stupid teenage things that got me into trouble. But Keri only sees me as this ogre who wants to make her suffer."

"I remember those teenage years with Damon. He didn't give me much trouble, but he and his father constantly bumped heads. For a while, the only thing they seemed to agree on was baseball. Where is my son, anyway?"

"Outside playing baseball with his sidekicks. I'm surprised you can't hear them with all the noise they're making. Let me get him for you." Audra opened the back door and poked her head out. Damon crouched in front of Junior, giving pointers on how to hold the bat.

"Damon, your mom's on the phone."

He looked up from his lowered position in front of their son. "Give me a few minutes."

"Did you hear that?" Audra asked, slipping back into the kitchen.

"I did. That must be an intense game."

Audra laughed. "Please, the kids love playing with him, but not one of them is athletic. Sadly, they all take after me."

Dena joined her in a hearty laugh.

Soon after, Damon entered the kitchen.

She handed him the phone, carefully ensuring their fingers didn't touch. The scent of sweat, grass, and outside clung to his skin, making her acutely aware of him—making her nostrils flare and her body turn on like a heated lamp. Physical exertion aroused her.

Damon sank onto one of the chairs at the table and wiped sweat from his brow with his forearm. "Hey, Ma."

As she drained the pasta in a colander, Audra listened to his side of the conversation. When he chuckled, the warm, easy sound fluttered through her insides and twinged her nipples.

Between her thighs throbbed at the thought of his big hands moving over her body in a knowing way. God, she wanted him. She had learned to tamp down her feelings because they didn't kiss or touch anymore, but she was starved for affection and fought hard to stifle the hunger that roared to life in his presence.

Some nights, she lay awake aching for him but didn't know how to move forward, chasing pleasure with a vibrator while her husband slept in a room down the hall. She piled pillows against her back to keep from feeling so alone in the bed, but they were a paltry substitute for the sensation of his firm, hard body behind her, and his soft snores lulling her to sleep after a bout of lovemaking.

Damon let out a low laugh. "All right Ma, hint, hint. I'll talk

29

to Audra, and we'll see what we can do, okay?" He fell silent, and when Audra glanced at him, she caught him staring at her ass.

His gaze lifted to hers, and her heart seized before speeding through her chest at the intent way he watched her, as if...

His attention shifted to the far wall as he continued the conversation. Had she misunderstood that look? Was that desire? She wasn't exactly dressed in sexy clothes. She wore knee-length shorts and a pale-yellow blouse that had seen better days.

Damon ended the call and stood. "She wants us to bring the kids out there for a week or two this summer."

"That's a good idea," Audra said, shoving her hands into pot holders and removing a tray of cheesy garlic bread from the oven.

"Last time they came out here, so I guess it's our turn to go see them."

She nodded and shifted the bread onto a platter. "When do you think?"

He shrugged. "Don't know. I guess we can play it by ear. Maybe after Tracy and Junior are finished with camp?"

They started day camp next week.

Audra nodded. "Sounds good."

"Okay." He turned toward the door.

"Could you call the kids in for dinner?" Audra asked.

"Sure."

He exited out the door, and she heard him calling the children. They all came in, and the four of them took turns washing up while she placed dinner on the table.

Soon, they were all seated together—a rarity nowadays. This moment exemplified the life she had wanted. The life they had agreed upon when they got married. A traditional family with Damon going to work and her taking care of the children and household. But she did not experience a sense of satisfaction.

As Damon bent his head and said grace, Audra lifted her eyes to him and fought the ache of longing that bloomed in her chest. Her nerves were close to snapping. How much longer could they go on like this?

Pretending they weren't struggling. Pretending they didn't live like mere acquaintances—instead of husband and wife.

Chapter Four

Parents and students filled Westerly Academy's auditorium for the end-of-year awards program. Damon and Audra sat near the front with Junior and Tracy between them. In the row behind them sat Audra's brother, Ethan, their mother, Rose, and Ethan's fiancée, Skye.

"The following students achieved all A's this year. Bianca Diaz!"

Audra waited impatiently for the principal to go down the short, alphabetical list of award recipients. Finally, he called her daughter's name.

"Kerilyn Walters!"

The auditorium erupted in applause. The family cheered and clapped, and Junior and Tracy jumped to their feet and hollered for their big sister.

Damon whistled. "Way to go, Keri!" He held a small video camera to his face to capture the moment.

The principal and Kerilyn faced the audience, her daughter holding her plaque with a broad smile. Heart swelling with pride, Audra snapped photos with her phone.

The program continued for another hour, with other students receiving awards for perfect attendance and exceptional work in specific subjects like foreign language, math, and science.

When the program ended, Kerilyn came over to them, her face bright and excited. Large curls bounced on her shoulders. Her firstborn looked all grown up in a black wrap dress and silver jewelry that sparkled against her skin.

"Let me see your award." Audra took the plaque, gazing at her daughter's name etched into the gold plate. "I'm so proud of you." She pulled Kerilyn into a one-arm hug.

"Keep up the good work," Rose said, squeezing Kerilyn's arm.

"Thanks, Grandma."

Ethan, tall and imposing in a three-piece suit because he came to the event directly from work, stepped forward. A multi-billionaire, he ran a real estate empire that spanned the globe.

"All A's is quite an accomplishment," he remarked.

Kerilyn's smile widened. "Advanced Physics almost messed me up, but I pulled out an "A" on the final, and that brought up my grade."

"Your mom told me that you wanted to find a part-time job this summer."

"I do." Kerilyn glanced at Audra. "You promised if I got good grades, I could get a job and make my own money, so I can buy whatever I want."

"Yes, I did."

"So, I still can, right?"

"Yes, you can." A deal was a deal, and Audra wouldn't renege on the promise she made to her daughter.

"Yay!" Kerilyn quietly squealed and did a shoulder bounce.

"If you're interested, I'm looking for a marketing assistant at

Connor Industries. The position is entry-level and full-time, not part-time. You'll work with the team promoting Horizon, my mixed-use community. Duties include working on our social media campaign and marketing literature like brochures, analyzing analytics, and doing whatever the managers need you to do. Sound like something you'd be interested in?"

Kerilyn's eyes widened. "Are you serious? Yes, I'm interested."

"You'll have a heavy workload," Ethan warned.

"I can handle it. Mom, can I? I know I said part-time, but full-time means I can make more money, and I'll be learning some cool stuff."

Audra pretended to hesitate. "Well, since it's your Uncle Ethan..."

"Oh my gosh, oh my gosh, thank you." Kerilyn ran in place, squealing. "I won't let you down, Uncle Ethan, I promise."

"I'm sure you won't since you made all A's. I'm expecting great work from you."

When Kerilyn first mentioned wanting a summer job, Audra and Damon discussed having Damon create a position for her at his company, but they quickly agreed that she'd probably be bored. He had a small office with a staff of two who helped him manage his affairs. That's when Audra put in a call to Ethan.

She gave her brother the details about Kerilyn's likes and dislikes and what she considered her daughter's top skills. A couple days later, Ethan called to say he had created a spot for her in the marketing department.

Thank you, Audra mouthed to her brother.

"I want a job," Tracy announced.

They all laughed.

Damon rested a hand on her shoulder. "No, you don't. For now, I'll buy whatever you need."

Skye looped her arm around Ethan's. "We better go."

He checked the time on his watch. "It's later than I thought. I have a business meeting in Las Vegas first thing in the morning, so we're flying out tonight," he explained.

"After they drop me off, so it's time for me to go too," Rose said.

"Thank you for coming. Have a safe flight," Audra said.

After hugs all around, Ethan, Rose, and Skye left them in the auditorium.

"What does the straight-A student want for dinner, to celebrate?" Damon asked.

Kerilyn screwed up her face in deep thought. "Umm."

"Pizza!" Junior yelled.

"I want pepperoni pizza," Tracy said, to no one's surprise. That was the only pizza she let past her lips.

"It's Keri's night," Audra gently reminded them. "She gets to pick. Where do you want to eat?"

Kerilyn took a look at her siblings' crestfallen faces. "I guess we can go for pizza."

"Yay!" the little ones screamed.

Despite being annoyed by her younger brother and sister at times, Kerilyn always watched out for them.

Audra smiled. "All right, let's go."

On their way out the auditorium, other parents stopped them several times to congratulate Kerilyn on a job well done. When they finally arrived outside, rain poured from the sky in heavy sheets, and people ducked into cars pulled up alongside the curb.

"I knew I should have brought in the umbrella," Damon muttered.

"It's raining really hard," Tracy said, pointing out the obvious.

"Y'all stay here. I'll get the car," Damon said.

"You'll get soaked," Audra told him.

"I parked halfway down the middle aisle. Shouldn't be bad. Unless you have a better idea."

"No," she admitted.

"Daddy, can I come with you?" Junior asked.

"You have to move fast," Damon said.

"I will."

From his excited grin, Audra guessed Junior simply wanted an excuse to play in the rain.

"I don't want to get wet." Tracy edged closer to Audra and took her hand.

"You won't. Daddy and Junior are going to get the car for us," Audra said.

"We'll be right back," Damon said.

He waited until a car passed by, and then he jogged into the parking lot with Junior beside him, his short legs pumping fast despite his father's slow run. They disappeared from sight for a few minutes, and then Damon's old-gold Range Rover appeared with the lights on.

He pulled up alongside the curb and hopped out with an umbrella, and Audra caught her breath at his appearance. Droplets of water dotted his face, and more water had soaked through his shirt and the undershirt in spots. The material clung to him and revealed the generosity of muscles in his arms and torso.

"Let's go, ladies." Damon popped open the back door. Holding the umbrella overhead, he helped Tracy into the vehicle. Kerilyn followed, and he closed the door behind them.

Then he faced Audra, and they watched each other awkwardly for a moment. Her stomach coiled into uncomfortable knots. She temporarily forgot the crowd of students and parents around them, waiting their turn to escape the pouring rain, and briefly considered telling him he didn't have to bother. But that seemed extreme.

Damon opened the door, and after a moment's hesitation, Audra slipped under the umbrella. Their arms brushed, and though he wore long sleeves, she experienced a charge that made her heart leap with excitement. As he guided her to the door, his fingers grazed the base of her spine, so featherlight she nearly missed it.

Her blood leapt at the faint touch, and she almost gave in to her natural inclination to seek closer contact. They touched so rarely nowadays, she lived for these moments because they were so few and far between.

But then his hand fell away, leaving her bereft and unsettled by his withdrawal.

When she sat in the seat, he closed the door and she watched him walk around to the driver side.

"All right, let's go get pizza," Damon announced, shifting the vehicle into gear.

"Pizza. Pizza. Pizza." Junior's excited chanting came from the backseat.

On the drive to the restaurant, Audra joined in the debate over which pizza they should order in addition to pepperoni, and whether they should get an order of the mozzarella sticks.

But she couldn't stop thinking about the brush of Damon's fingers along the base of her spine. Strange to think that over a year ago, touching each other was as ordinary an act as breathing. Everything changed between them for an intensely private, heart-breaking reason very few were privy to.

Three miscarriages in two years. Individually, they recovered from the pain of loss, but their relationship didn't. The marriage became... broken, for lack of a better word. Their hopes and dreams died a little with each loss, and the glow of marriage transformed into tarnished brass, atrophied and dying a slow death.

Chapter Five

The family filed into the house from the garage, bellies full of soda, pepperoni pizza, and an all-meat pizza. They all indulged in the post meal dessert of warm brownies topped with ice cream, except for Tracy. She wanted only ice cream because she couldn't tolerate her brownie getting soaked with melting ice cream. Kerilyn and Damon ate an entire dessert each, while Junior and Audra shared one between them.

"Everybody get upstairs and get ready for bed. It's late and you have school in the morning." Audra rested her Coach purse on the island.

Clutching her award against her chest, Kerilyn stood across from Audra, a wide grin on her face. "Mom, Dad," she said.

"Yes, baby," Audra said, mind running through the list of tasks to complete before she went upstairs.

"I have a job."

Audra hadn't seen her daughter this happy in a long time. Her entire face lit up in a bright smile, eyes glowing with excitement and anticipation.

"Yes, you do," Damon said with some amusement.

"You better do a good job for your Uncle Ethan," Audra said.

"I will. I know he's tough, and I won't let him down. This is going to be the best summer *ever*. I have a summer job, hey. I have a summer job, hey. I have a summer job..."

She sang the words as she danced out the kitchen, and Tracy and Junior followed behind, mimicking her hand gestures and hip action.

"Should I be offended?" Damon asked. "I thought I gave her a pretty good allowance."

Audra let out a little laugh. "You're witnessing the naiveness of youth. She thinks she's going to be rich now."

Damon chuckled. "Guess I can't blame her. My first job, I just knew I was balling. I'll never forget seeing how much taxes the government took out. That hurt."

"We need to make sure she knows to budget and save, skills I learned the hard way after squandering my paychecks."

She'd been so spoiled growing up in a wealthy household, after she got a job, she consistently ran out of money and had to ask her mother and stepfather to cover nonessentials like make up—which were supposed to come out of her paycheck. Only after they had a talk with her did she get serious about managing her money instead of carelessly spending on makeup, clothes, and eating out, as if she had an infinite amount of cash.

"I'll take her to open an account one day next week before or after work. Give her the full experience of walking into a bank and opening her own account," Damon said.

"Oh, that's perfect. She'll love that."

Quiet descended on the room, a painfully awkward silence that dominated their moments alone. Audra shifted from one foot to the other, and Damon rubbed a hand along the back of his neck, a clear indication of his unease. Conversation proved difficult because they had little else to talk about but their children.

"I, uh, I'm going to check my email and then scan the refrigerator and pantry before I send in tomorrow's grocery order. Anything you need me to add to the list?" Audra asked.

"No, I'm good. If I think of anything, I'll pick up what I need one day when I'm out. I'm gonna head up."

"Okay."

Damon tapped his knuckles on the island top and headed out the interior French doors with a slow, ambling walk.

He's staying in tonight. Her shoulders lowered with released worry. She was way too eager and hungry for a bit of his attention. Obsessed.

She relived the way he touched her in the rain. His blunt fingertips grazed the base of her spine and created chaos in every corner of her body. The heat of that contact remained. Faint and light but ever present, like a dark shadow on her skin.

Audra took a deep breath and shook off the cobwebs of her thoughts.

She checked the refrigerator and pantry and then used the app to add a few items to the order. Then she went into the den to check email because she didn't like having email on her phone. Anyone who needed to reach her urgently could do so by text. Everyone else would have to wait.

Her mouse gliding over the pad, she breezed past communications she deemed nonessential. Delete. Delete. Delete. Midway down the list, she paused and hovered over a familiar name. The caretaker of their vacation property in the Dominican Republic.

"Regarding the roof." She read the subject line aloud before double-clicking and frowning as she read the body of the message.

The roof had sprung a leak.

41

She made a mental note to discuss the issue with Damon before she responded. She was the point of contact for their vacation homes—that one and the cabin in Wyoming. Decorating them had been a source of joy, and seeing Damon's jaw-dropping reaction at the transformations had filled her with a sense of pride.

While she took care of the personal properties, he was the point of contact for the income-generating properties managed by a company out of Atlanta, which oversaw their apartment complexes and commercial leasing space.

She made her way upstairs where Junior and Tracy's shrieks of laughter spilled from the open doorway of their bedroom. In another year or so, they would graduate to their own rooms, but for now, having them together made bedtime and morning routines easier to manage.

At the door, she noted the disarray in the room. Rumpled bed sheets and toys strewn about every corner of the room. Damon wrestled with Tracy and Junior on the floor. Junior had his father in a headlock, but she wasn't sure what Tracy was trying to do. She tugged one of her father's legs, as if trying to drag him across the floor. Damon wore the same shirt and slacks from earlier, but they had changed into their pajamas.

At the sight of Damon's animated face and the sound of his deep-throated laughter, a twinge of envy nicked her chest. He was made to be a father and clearly enjoyed every minute he spent with their kids.

Sorrow clenched her heart. They had both wanted a large family, but not once, not twice, but three times her body betrayed her and broke their hearts. The nursery remained untouched with the door locked so they wouldn't have to relive their grief. And the hole in her heart remained as glaringly empty as the extra bedrooms in their large home.

Damon rolled onto his back, dragging Junior and Tracy

with him. The second his eyes landed on Audra, she straightened and affixed a mild smile to her lips.

"Uh-oh, Mommy's here," he said.

"Uh-oh," the kids repeated.

"Am I right in assuming those two haven't brushed their teeth yet?"

"Five more minutes, Mommy," Tracy said.

"Yes, five more minutes," Junior pleaded with puppy-dog eyes.

Damon must have read the disapproving expression on her face because he sat up with them in his arms.

"Mommy said it's time to brush your teeth, so you gotta go brush your teeth."

He turned them toward the bathroom and patted their bottoms to shove them in that direction. They groaned, dragging their feet as they went to complete their nightly ritual.

Damon hopped to his feet and started picking up their toys, and Audra went into the closet to set out their clothes for school the next day.

When she came out, Damon lay on his back across Junior's bed with his eyes closed. She almost asked if he was okay or if he was tired. She didn't though. They weren't that type of couple anymore. They didn't ask questions about each other's well-being.

She walked across the carpeted floor to the adjoining bathroom and could almost swear his eyes followed her, but she didn't bother to check. She made sure Junior and Tracy did a good job brushing their teeth and then herded them back into the bedroom.

Audra sat Tracy on the side of the bed so she could work on one of her twists that had come undone.

Junior flopped across his father's stomach, and Damon emitted a pained groan.

43

"Can you fly me like Superman before I go to sleep?" the eight-year-old asked.

"Sure. We'll make two rounds."

Tracy swung her head in their direction, jerking her hair from Audra's fingers.

"I want a turn," she said.

"I'll give you a turn when your mom is finished with your hair," Damon promised.

He pushed off the bed and held their son horizontal over his head, with Junior's arms and legs stretched out like Superman. Then Junior "flew" around the room as Damon carried him.

"Watch out for that eagle." Damon took Junior into a sharp curve to avoid the imaginary bird.

"Uh-oh, here comes a jumbo jet filled with passengers." He dipped their son lower to avoid the imaginary plane. The entire time, Junior remained focused, arms and legs stretched taut.

Damon had been playing this game with them since they were toddlers. Initially, Audra worried about them falling and getting hurt, but they barely moved, comfortable and fearless in their father's hands.

While Junior flew around the room, she secured the end of Tracy's hair with more beads and then placed a bonnet on her head.

As soon as she finished, Tracy hopped off the bed and lifted her arms high to Damon. "My turn!"

Damon brought in Junior for a landing and lifted Tracy off her feet. She flew around the room in the same manner as her brother, except she became vocal whenever they encountered an obstacle.

"Get out the way," she screamed at the invisible bird and screeched when she almost ran into the imaginary jet.

Finally, Damon deposited her safely on her feet.

"All right, Superwoman, let's get you tucked in," Audra said.

Tracy scrambled into the bed. "Good night," she said, hugging the blue stuffed rabbit she slept with every night.

As Audra tucked the top sheet around her daughter, she heard Junior ask, "Daddy, are you in the doghouse?"

Her head twisted in that direction.

Damon paused in the midst of tucking in Junior. "Why did you ask me that?"

"Because we saw you sleeping on the sofa," Junior answered.

Last Saturday, he and Tracy had gone downstairs before Audra woke up and found their father asleep in the den. They woke him up and asked for breakfast. She assumed they had forgotten about the incident, but apparently not.

"How do you know the term 'doghouse'?" Damon asked.

"I heard it on YouTube."

"You watch a lot of YouTube. I'm going to have to take away your tablet."

"No, please don't," Junior said.

Damon straightened. "I'm not in the doghouse. I accidentally fell asleep watching TV on the sofa. Now you go to sleep. You talk too much."

Junior giggled, unperturbed by Damon's comment. "Good night, Daddy."

Audra came over and gave him a good-night kiss. "Good night, baby."

Damon left the room, but she made another visual sweep before she turned off the light and followed him out.

Chapter Six

S tanding side by side at the double vanity in their bathroom, Audra and Damon brushed their teeth in silence, avoiding eye contact in the mirror.

Damon finished before she did and exited the bathroom, while Audra quickly washed her face. When she went into the bedroom, Damon came out of his closet in pajamas.

Would he sleep in their bedroom tonight, or would he make an excuse to go downstairs and leave her alone?

"The caretaker at the property in the Dominican Republic sent an email," Audra said, rubbing hand cream into her fingers and palms. "The roof sprang a leak. He has someone who can fix it, but there's not enough in the account to cover the cost."

"You can transfer some money from the Citibank account," Damon said.

"I wasn't sure if that's what you wanted me to do. I'll do that tomorrow."

He frowned. "I need to go down there one weekend to check on the property."

He said, "I."

Not *we*.

Audra padded over to the bed. "That's a good idea. It's been awhile."

Spring break of last year they visited the property and had discussed going this year, but their plans changed.

"I'm going downstairs to watch TV."

Again, she thought. Disappointment soured in her belly.

Going downstairs to watch TV had become Damon's ritual on the nights he didn't stay out late, as if he couldn't stand to lie next to her. If he didn't fall asleep downstairs, he came upstairs and slept in one of the spare bedrooms. She never asked him why, but one day, he shared that he did that because he didn't want to disturb her rest. *Yeah, right.*

"Okay."

Audra didn't know what else to say, short of begging and pleading with him to spend more than one night a week in bed with her. Pretending she didn't care, she climbed under the covers.

"You want the lights off?" Damon asked.

"Yes. Thanks."

He flipped the switch and left. In the silent darkness, Audra sank lower in the bed and turned onto her side, resting her head on Damon's pillow. A hint of masculine spice invaded her nostrils from the last time he'd slept in their bed, and she drew in a deep breath to receive even more.

In happier times, Damon smiled often and couldn't keep his hands off her. Like one night when they went out to dinner to celebrate a licensing deal he had signed with a juice company. They had hired a car to go out, and when they were ready to leave, the driver returned to the restaurant, picked them up, and dropped them off at home.

The entire night, Audra had mercilessly teased Damon by

playing footsie under the table and sprinkling double entendres into their conversations.

In the back of the Lincoln town car, she rubbed his thigh and accidentally on purpose brushed his crotch. The minute his eyes snapped to her, though he didn't say a word, she knew she was in trouble.

When they entered the foyer of their home, he was at his breaking point. He pulled her into his arms.

Biting his bottom lip, Damon's languorous eyes gazed down at her. "You like teasing me, huh?"

"Moi? I don't know what you mean." She wanted him so much her panties were damp.

"You knew exactly what you were doing. Made me so damn horny, I almost spread you on the table and ate you instead of my meal." He whispered the words, taking a second to nip her bottom lip with his teeth.

"You're so nasty," Audra said, wrapping her arms around his torso.

"You like it."

She did.

He nibbled her earlobe, and she giggled, pressing her body flat against his.

On the way up the stairs, Damon's hands and mouth roamed Audra's body, and she kissed him with enthusiasm, horny and eager to screw.

They stumbled into the bedroom with panting laughter.

"I love when you look at me like that," Damon whispered.

"Like what?"

"Like you can't wait for me to fuck you."

"That's because I can't."

He released a guttural groan and hastily hauled off her

clothes, then his, tossing them into a heap on the floor beside the bed. His hand curled around her nape, and he hauled her to him, his mouth descending into a consuming kiss.

He plundered her lips in a raw, demanding way. The hard pressure and probing caress of his tongue liquefied her knees and forced her to cling to his broad shoulders. She strained against him like a needy harlot, sliding her hands up his neck and into his tight curls to anchor his mouth against hers.

Lips fused together, Damon lifted her from the floor, his fingers digging into her plump bottom as she curled her legs around him. They went down on the bed together, and he covered her body with his, almost his full weight resting on top of her.

One hand slipped between her thighs. His fingers stroked her damp folds, and she moaned as desire burned a path through her veins. His touch was intoxicating, his mouth a drugging caress as it strayed to the hollow at the base of her throat. Writhing atop the sheets, Audra smoothed her palms over the defined muscles of his back to his tight ass.

Damon kissed her cheek and chin and gave the same attention to her shoulders before dipping lower to her large breasts. Her nipples tightened with the silken stroke of his tongue, and she angled her hips higher as his touch drew whimpers from her throat.

She nipped at his ear, dragging in a lungful of his spicy, masculine scent. Mindless with need, she parted her legs wider in an urgent plea for his possession. His hard length pressed against her thigh, long and thick and exquisitely hard.

"Damon." His name was a raw, desperate sound on her lips.

At that moment, she wasn't a wife or mother. She was simply a woman begging her lover to give the ultimate pleasure.

Damon traveled lower. His beard scraped the curve of her soft belly, a tantalizing contrast to the soft texture of his mouth.

When his lips grazed the strip of hair in the middle of her mons, she sucked in a deep breath. He teased her clit, his talented tongue dragging cries of bliss from the depths of her throat. She bucked her hips into his mouth and gripped the back of his head.

She came suddenly and hard, the climax hitting her with wave after wave of pleasure. Her cries increased in intensity as he relentlessly tongued her drenched flesh, wringing yet another orgasm from her trembling body.

When he finally lifted away from her, Damon licked her juices off his lips and crawled up the bed, his dark eyes intent. He didn't give her time to descend from the sexual high. His tongue danced over the peaks of her breasts, and he sprinkled hot kisses in between the valley of the soft mounds.

His stiff erection butted against her core, and she moaned her delight, ready for his next move with dizzying anticipation. Damon pinned her wrists above her head with one hand, and her legs splayed wide to welcome him in. Holding his shaft in the other hand, he guided his body into hers with a hard thrust.

Audra gasped. She twisted, desperate to touch him, but he had her hands pinned to the pillows. She pulled her knees into her chest, and he rocked deeper into her body.

"This right here is... heaven," he breathed in a strained voice.

Audra couldn't agree more. Their bodies fit together as if they were made for each other.

In the dim light, his handsome face tightened. When he caught her staring, he captured her lips with his and flicked his tongue against the roof of her mouth.

"I want to touch you," Audra whispered.

Damon released her wrists, and she wound her arms around his neck. His chest hairs teased the tips of her breasts with each gliding motion. Every movement, every sensation, felt incredible.

Caged in between his muscular arms while he stroked in and out of her, she arched her throat into his damp kisses. Her *legs closed around his waist and she tightened her feminine muscles around him. Immediately, his rhythm stuttered, and he groaned at the intensified tightness.*

The leisurely rhythm was abandoned and replaced by his hips jerking harder. His breathing came faster and harsher in her ear. Oh, how she loved when he lost control.

As another climax built in her loins, Audra closed her eyes and tightened her arms around his neck. "I love you, honey... Damon, oh Damon, Damon, Damon."

He buried his face in the side of her neck and used one hand beneath her bottom to pull her into his hard strokes.

Audra begged him to go harder, and he angled his hips so he hit the perfect spot. With a hoarse cry, she came with a severity that left her blindly clawing at his damp back. She buried her face into the wet, salty skin of his neck. Clinging to him, she held on and continued pumping her hips until he also came.

Damon shuddered through the orgasm with a guttural groan before he lost all his strength and collapsed on top of her.

Audra jerked back to reality from her erotic memory.

That particular night had been one of the last times they simply had sex for the sake of having sex, without the pressure of pregnancy hovering in the back of her mind and tamping her desire.

She lay on her back with the sheets tangled around her legs. Her entire body ached—between her legs, her breasts. Even her hair follicles seemed to beg for relief.

She turned onto her side and squeezed her thighs together, and with the friction against her wet, swollen sex, she came instantly. Her fingers curled into the soft sheets, and she buried her face in Damon's pillow to stifle the husky cries.

Afterward, she moaned her frustration. Coming in that

way took the edge off and satisfied her temporarily but wasn't the same as Damon's hands and mouth on her body. There was no one to cuddle with afterward either. No one to idly caress her body in an affectionate way.

With a burst of anger, Audra shoved his pillows to the floor and fluffed her own. She tugged the blanket higher and closed her eyes.

Tomorrow, she was changing the sheets.

Chapter Seven

Tracy came skipping into the kitchen. "Look, Mommy. Keri helped me."

She had added pink ribbons to her hair.

"I like that. You look pretty, baby." Audra dropped containers into a tote bag as Junior and Kerilyn walked into the room. "Are we all set?"

"All set," Kerilyn said.

"What about Daddy?" Tracy asked.

"Daddy has to work late."

"Aww."

"I know, we'll all miss him, but we'll still have fun. Everybody will be there."

"Grandma and *Abuelo*?" Tracy asked with a hopeful lilt to her voice.

"Yes. And Auntie Monica, and Uncle Thiago, and everybody. So come on, let's go," Audra said.

She ushered the children into her white Mercedes S-class, and before long, they were on their way to Bruno's house on the outskirts of the city. They arrived early, but cars were already in the driveway, including Ethan's limousine and her sister Monica's yellow Ferrari.

The large, one-story home on a basement was located north of the city. Light spilled from the windows all the way to the double doors, which allowed visitors to see inside as they approached.

Audra turned the doorknob and entered the house. "We're here!"

Tracy and Junior raced ahead toward the den, and she heard cries of excitement as they encountered family members. Kerilyn followed more slowly.

Audra walked into the newly designed kitchen, eyes sweeping over the array of food options. Tonight's menu consisted of steak and duck. The tempting scent of roasting meat and a plethora of delicious sides filled the air and made her mouth water.

She loved the changes Bruno had made. New appliances, lighting fixtures, floors, and granite countertops refreshed the space. Despite adding a giant island with a sink in the middle, the kitchen appeared larger and brighter. For her chef brother, the changes would definitely inspire new ideas.

Audra soon discovered almost everyone had arrived early. The only people missing were Monica's new boyfriend—or old boyfriend made new again, since they originally met in college —and Ignacio.

"You're sure Andre is coming?" she asked her sister, who was cute in a silver peasant dress and silver chandelier earrings. Monica wore her hair in a short natural cut close to her scalp.

Audra lifted a carrot from the vegetable tray on the counter. Bruno had prepared hors d'oeuvres for them to munch on until dinner.

"I'm positive. He's coming."

"Who's coming, Auntie Monica?" Tracy asked.

"My friend, Andre. He'll be here soon." Monica playfully tugged on one of her niece's twists.

"He's eating dinner with us?"

"He sure is."

"I can't wait to meet him," Audra said.

"Be nice," Monica warned.

Audra laughed. "You don't have to worry about me. You need to worry about our brothers."

Monica groaned. "I know."

Audra laughed again and took the vegetable tray as she left the kitchen. She sauntered to the outdoor dining area, which the contractors had also renovated. They repaired the patio and overlaid the cement slab with colorful handmade tiles from Mexico.

Lights strewn across the pergola lit up the outdoors, but not too much, allowing for an intimate scene. In addition to a large grill, Bruno had added a pizza oven. Outdoor sofas for reclining were on one side and encouraged conversation.

She placed the tray next to the other snacks on a side table while Bruno and her stepfather, Benicio Santana, pushed together two tables to accommodate their large family. Benicio had a head full of white hair and a white beard. Bruno had dark hair and his father's gray eyes.

Audra helped them place chairs under the tables.

"Did you hire any help?" she asked.

Bruno checked his watch. "I did. Two servers. They should be here any minute. I need to check on the duck." He hurried inside.

"I'm going to fix myself a plate and take one to your mother. Is she in the kitchen?" Benicio asked.

"She moved to the den," Audra answered.

Her stepfather nodded, fixed a plate of hors d'oeuvres, and

disappeared into the house.

She inhaled deeply and gazed up at the stars. Because her brother lived outside the city, they were evident in the black night sky. Nearby, Thiago slowly walked the area beside the outdoor sofas, head down as he quietly talked to someone on the phone.

Unlike Bruno and Ignacio, he'd inherited his mother's dark eyes, which combined with his black hair and full beard gave him a brooding, smoldering look.

Audra dipped a stalk of celery in Bruno's homemade blue cheese dressing and took a bite.

Thiago sighed, shaking his head as he tucked the phone in his pocket.

"Business?" she asked.

"Sí, unfortunately," he answered in accented English, his thick eyebrows lowered over his eyes.

"I hope you resolved the problem. You know how Mom gets about using the phone during family time."

Audra was the same way, though not as rigid as her mother. No phones at the table allowed.

"I know. That's why I wanted to hurry and get it taken care of. Unfortunately, some people think because they pay you for a service, they own your time, all the time."

"I remember having to deal with that when I worked at Benicio's company. I don't have that problem anymore, thank goodness."

Before she married Damon, she had worked in her stepfather's office as an administrative assistant, fully expecting to rise in the ranks of the company. However, getting pregnant with Junior and a quick marriage at the courthouse had put the kibosh on her career aspirations. Only after Tracy was a toddler did she start working again, this time blogging and turning Plush into a business that generated a little income.

"Lucky you."

She stepped closer to her brother and lowered her voice. "Have you talked to him about taking over the company?"

Thiago glanced over his shoulder to make sure they were alone. "More than once."

"And...?"

He shook his head in disgust. "Nothing has changed. He's not interested. He is determined to continue working full-time."

After a successful career in acting, Benicio expanded his personal fortune by investing in real estate, retail establishments, and a popular tequila brand bottled in his native Mexico. The consulting arm of the conglomerate offered other businesses the opportunity to learn from his many years of knowledge.

"I don't understand why, when you're willing to take over. You know the company inside out, not only the consulting arm. You would be the perfect person to take the reins of Benicio's company, if he ever retires."

"That's not important to him."

"Why not? His work schedule caused him to lose his wife, for goodness' sake."

"My father is a very stubborn man, in case you haven't noticed," Thiago said in a dry tone.

"Oh, I've noticed. Why do you think he's like that?"

He fell quiet, frowning as he considered the question. "I think it's because of my mother."

"What does Valentina have to do with it? They've been divorced for ages."

"My mother was very spoiled and used to getting what she wanted. She made a lot of demands on my father, and I believe —I don't know this for sure—his stubborn behavior is a way of rebelling against the same thing happening again. Yes, he loves to work, but this insistence on doing it, no matter what, doesn't make sense."

"Particularly since he's a smart man."

Thiago nodded his agreement.

"So, what are you going to do?"

He shrugged, continuing to frown. "I'm working on him."

"Good luck."

He laughed softly, a wordless way to acknowledge he had a lot of work to do.

"Is Damon coming tonight?"

Audra glanced away. She hated lying to her family. "No, he had to work."

Thiago's gaze practically burned a hole in the side of her face. When she finally glanced at him again, she saw blatant skepticism.

"Don't look at me like that."

"No one believes that excuse anymore."

Her eyes widened. "Have you guys been talking about me?"

He shrugged, which basically meant yes.

She closed her eyes and groaned. "Who?"

"Me, Bruno, Ethan."

"Oh god." She covered her face.

"We *care* about you," Thiago said.

"I know. I..." Audra shook her head. "There's a lot going on."

"Like what?"

Audra pushed frustrated air past her lips. "Damon and I are going through a difficult period. We'll figure it out."

"What does that mean, 'a difficult period'?"

"We're not communicating, and he's gone a lot. Most nights we don't even sleep in the same bed."

Thiago's thick eyebrows dropped lower over his eyes. "Do

you think he's having an affair?"

"I don't know. Maybe."

His face hardened. Oh boy, she should have never said anything like that to him. Thiago was a hothead.

Audra placed a hand on his arm. "Thiago, I don't know *for sure.*"

His features softened as he brought his temper under control. "Have you tried talking to him?"

She let out a mirthless laugh. "Damon doesn't talk. I think it's because of what happened when he was younger."

"The abuse?"

She nodded. "He clams up. Right now, he's distant, and I don't know how to get past the barrier between us. I feel lost. Helpless."

She refrained from adding how frightened she was of hearing the truth from Damon. If he told her what was wrong, she might not be able to handle the unvarnished honesty of his list of grievances.

"If you love each other, you should work it out. Don't be stubborn like our parents."

Audra gave him a rueful smile. "I won't."

Her brother pulled her into his side. "Whenever you need to talk, I'm here."

"I know. Thank you."

Audra rested her head against his shoulder, realizing her great fortune. She had a wonderful, caring family and could talk to any one of its members about her predicament, but she always hesitated. Embarrassment, shame, denial instead of facing reality, all held her back.

She and Thiago remained outside talking, then Ignacio arrived and Kerilyn strolled out, head bent over her phone, as usual. Later, Andre and Monica came outside, and her sister introduced him to everyone. A good-looking guy with slightly narrowed eyes, he studied them all as if he wasn't quite sure he wanted to be there.

The family gathered around the table, and Benicio stood at the head, surveying them with a slight smile on his face.

"Everyone is here, yes?" he asked.

"Except Maxwell," Monica said.

A series of moans filled the table. Maxwell, the youngest, was completing his residency out of state. Audra hoped he moved back after he finished, but he could end up taking a job somewhere else.

"And me." A male voice came from the direction of the door leading into the house.

They all turned, and Audra's breath caught in her throat when Damon strolled toward them.

"Daddy!" Tracy screamed, almost jumping out of her chair with excitement.

Damon stopped next to Bruno's chair, holding a bottle of wine in a wine bag. His face broke into a smile that made her heart stop.

"Looks like I arrived just in time," he said.

Everyone started talking at once because they hadn't seen him in a while. He smiled and nodded at the welcoming chorus of voices, but Audra remained silent. Why did he come when he said he wouldn't?

Thiago shot a questioning glance at her. She shot back a don't-you-dare-say-anything look. He arched an eyebrow but held his tongue. He and Ethan then shifted their chairs so Damon could squeeze in across from her.

Taking a sip of water, she eyed her husband over the rim. As he sat down, their gazes met and she shot him a weak smile.

"Okay, let's try this again," Benicio said, and they all laughed. "Let us pray."

The family held hands, and he blessed the food.

Chapter Eight

Bruno entered the kitchen with an empty glass, and Audra smoothed a hand over the granite countertop. "I know I've already told you, but I absolutely love the changes you made. I'm a little jealous, to be honest, and you've given me ideas for what I can do at our house."

His gray eyes, so much like his father's, crinkled at the corners when he smiled. He placed the glass in the sink. "I didn't know you planned to make changes to your kitchen."

"I didn't plan to, but seeing your changes has inspired me."

Bruno rested a hip against the massive island. "Be prepared to spend a lot of time on the project. I should have cloned myself."

"You *should* have slowed down and taken a break. You've earned the time off."

He nodded in agreement. "You're right, I need to take a break. I've been so busy for a long time, only taking a few days here and there. I should take a real vacation. For a couple of weeks at least, but I can't seem to slow down."

"That's your Santana genes. You're like your father, but we

all need to recharge. As far as I'm concerned, vacations are part of self-care."

"You're so much smarter than me," Bruno said.

"After all these years, you're only now figuring that out?" Audra teased.

Before Bruno could give a snappy answer in return, Damon entered the kitchen.

Bruno glanced surreptitiously at Audra. "Damon, glad you could make it. Audra said you weren't coming," he said evenly.

Audra busied packing up some of the leftovers, the task she came into the kitchen to complete.

"I didn't think I'd be able to at first. Audra told me about the changes to the kitchen weeks ago, so I did my best to get here. Plus, I look forward to your delicious meals."

Bruno laughed, but she knew her brother well enough to recognize the tension in his laughter. She was very close to her family, and her brothers were protective.

"I appreciate the compliment. I hope we'll see you at family events more often. Seems work has kept you busy of late," Bruno remarked.

Audra shot a warning glance at him. She didn't need him to fight her battles or whatever he called himself doing.

"Yeah, it has," Damon said, tension entering his own voice.

Bruno shot him a tight smile. "I know all about that. Excuse me, I need to finish cleaning up outside." With one final look at Audra, he strolled out of the kitchen.

In the silence, Damon's gaze bored into her back.

"Tracy fell asleep watching a movie with your mom. I can take her to the car for you."

Audra snapped the cover on a container of vegetables. "Thank you. I'm actually ready to go."

She placed the containers into her tote bag and slowly turned to face Damon.

"What did you say to your brother?" he asked in a lowered voice.

"Nothing."

"Nothing?" He arched a skeptical eyebrow.

"That's right. Nothing."

"He was acting kind of weird."

"That's your imagination."

His eyes narrowed. "I'm not an idiot, Audra. You've clearly been badmouthing me to your family."

"I have *not*. He's my brother. You know how they are, they're protective."

"So, you admit you said something?"

At the end of her rope, she glared at him. How dare he question her?

"What is there to say? Would you like me to tell my family that we barely talk and most nights we don't sleep in the same bed? Don't worry, our secrets are safe with me. As far as they know, we're the epitome of marital bliss." That wasn't entirely true because she had opened up to Thiago, but Damon didn't need to know that.

He blew air through his nose, as if he didn't believe her, tension coiling off him with the density of fog. "No way they believe that, at least not after tonight. It was very obvious you didn't want me here."

"I have no problem with you being here, but you said you weren't coming."

"You sure you don't have a problem with me being here? Because your face said something different at dinner."

"That was my surprised face."

"That's all?"

Audra let out an exasperated sigh. "Not now, Damon."

"Not now? You're the one who always wants to talk. Why isn't now a good time?"

"You really think right now, at my brother's house is the right time to have this conversation? You're obviously itching for a fight. I'm sorry I didn't jump for joy when you arrived, but I didn't expect you to be here. I point blank asked if you were coming, and you said no. Had you been honest, we could have come here in one vehicle, as a family. You made me look as if I don't know my own husband's plans."

"I changed my mind at the last minute."

"Whose fault is that?" Audra hissed. "Look, I don't want to argue with you in Bruno's kitchen—"

"I don't want to argue either, but I wish you'd be honest and just... say it."

"Say what?"

"Say you don't want me here."

"I don't know what you're talking about." Audra started for the door, but Damon stepped in front of her.

She pulled up short as anger billowed between them.

Right at that moment, Monica pranced into the kitchen with a big smile on her face. "Hey, you two."

Her boyfriend sauntered in behind her.

By her sister's flushed face and Andre's wrinkled shirt, they'd probably been getting busy somewhere in the house. Lucky Monica. She received affection and attention, which Audra craved.

"Hey," Audra said in a low voice.

The happiness on Monica's face disappeared as she switched her gaze between them. "Everything okay?"

"Everything is fine," Damon said in a clipped voice.

Audra forced a smile to her face. "Andre, it was nice to meet you. I've gotta get my children so we can go. Excuse me." She walked by Damon and went into the living room on shaky legs.

Say you don't want me here.

64

True, she didn't want him there, but not for the reason he thought. His presence meant having to give explanations to family members. Thiago already thought it odd that she didn't know her own husband was going to be there, and other family members—like Monica and Bruno—detected the tension between them.

She found Tracy fast asleep on the sofa, leaning against her mother, Rose. A slender, dark-skinned woman, Rose had an arm around Tracy while she watched television. Meanwhile, Junior fought sleep on the floor, lying on his side with one of the sofa pillows cushioning his head, eyes fluttering closed and then flying open at the last minute.

Audra held out a hand to her son. "Come on baby, time to go."

Junior sat up, yawning and stretching. She took his hand and pulled him to his feet.

"What about this little angel?" Rose asked.

"Damon is coming to get her."

Right as the words left her mouth, her husband entered the room.

"She's out cold," Rose said with amusement in her voice, stealing a quick squeeze.

"I'll take her off your hands." Damon lifted his daughter away from her grandmother, and Tracy let out a quiet mewl but barely moved as he settled her head on his shoulder.

Rose yawned. "I might have to take a nap myself. I'm exhausted."

"Since you don't have your driver, do you need me to take you home?" Audra asked.

"No, I'm fine," her mother said.

"Then you should stay the night and save yourself a trip if you're sleepy."

"I came with Ben. I'll see if he wants to stay the night or not. You all drive carefully."

"You too. Good night, Mom." Audra kissed her mother's cheek.

Before she could pull away, her mother's fingers circled her arm, and they locked eyes.

"Are you okay?" Rose asked in a quiet voice.

Her mother was no fool, but Audra placed a fake smile on her face and lied to her anyway. "I'm fine."

"Good night, Grandma." Junior squeezed between them and flung himself at Rose.

"Good night, my love." Rose embraced him in a tight hug, patting his back and kissing his cheek. "Damon, good to see you tonight. We've missed you."

"Work and other commitments have kept me busy," Damon replied from across the room.

"Well, hopefully things are starting to change."

Damon only nodded, as Rose's very astute eyes remained on his face.

Audra pulled Junior closer. He mumbled something as he slipped an arm around her waist, leaning heavily into her side, definitely ready for bed.

She and Damon said goodbye to the rest of the family in the backyard. Then they left with Kerilyn pulling up the rear, slowly walking to the Mercedes in the driveway.

Junior climbed in the back and snapped on his seatbelt, eyes droopy. Before they arrived at home, he would be fast asleep.

Damon placed Tracy in the car seat and strapped her in, and Kerilyn climbed in the front seat.

Audra turned to him. "Are you coming straight home?" she asked in a low voice.

To her ears that was a ridiculous question to ask her own husband, but his late nights meant he might not.

"You need help getting Junior and Tracy out the car, so yes. I'll be right behind you."

She hated herself a little bit for the relief that flooded her system. She didn't know where he went at nights, but at least if he came home, he wasn't elsewhere with God knows who.

"I'll see you at the house then."

"Yeah."

He walked in the direction of his SUV, and she climbed into her car.

In the past, Damon wouldn't allow her to open a car door herself. Those small, considerate gestures no longer existed between them. They lived like people who barely knew each other.

It hurt like hell.

Chapter Nine

Benicio walked into the living room and found Rose curled on the sofa, head pillowed on the armrest, fast asleep. He watched her for a moment, a smile lifting the corners of his lips. She could fall asleep just about anywhere.

With the rest of the family gone and the house mostly quiet, the only sounds came from Bruno and his staff in the kitchen.

Benicio brushed a strand of hair from his ex-wife's cheek. When they first met, she wore her hair longer, but over the years, she'd cut it shorter and shorter. Now the dark strands dipped a couple of inches past her shoulders, streaked with gray. Nonetheless, she looked like the young mother he ran into at the grocery store decades ago. With a toddler on her hip, she shepherded her two older children into the backseat of the car. She'd accidentally bumped the shopping cart, which contained bags of groceries and started across the parking lot toward another car.

He sprang into action and grabbed the wayward cart,

bringing it back to her. She had been extremely grateful, and despite her harried expression and her wearing a T-shirt stained with mustard, he was smitten. Had he not stopped at the store that day, had he asked a member of his staff to pick up the items he wanted, he would have never run into Rose—or as he called her, Rosa. He would have never known the joy of being loved by her and loving her. Truly the best years of his life.

Benicio took her hand and gently squeezed. She lifted her head and blinked.

"Oh my goodness, what time is it?"

"Very late. Everyone has gone."

"I fell asleep, didn't I?"

She yawned and stretched, breasts lifting higher in the blouse she wore. For a second, his body tightened with need. Over time, he put on a couple dozen pounds, but she remained as slim as the day they met.

"Bruno is putting away the food. Did you want to take anything with you?" he asked.

"I'll take some of the duck, if he has any left."

"I believe he does. Let's see." Benicio extended his hand and helped her to her feet, holding on a little longer than necessary before letting go.

They strolled into the kitchen, where Bruno—his eldest biological son and the one who looked most like him—busied cleaning up the kitchen with a member of his staff.

"You're awake," Bruno said, smiling.

"Barely. Obviously, I'm more tired than I realized," Rose said.

"Well, it is late. Did you want to take any food with you?"

"Do you have any that delicious duck left?"

"I do. I'll put some in a container for you and include some sides."

"Perfect."

Benicio had already told his son he didn't want any of the leftovers, so he waited patiently while Bruno prepared the container and then handed it to Rose.

"Thank you, baby. I love the changes you made. I know you'll be happier now."

"Very," Bruno confirmed.

Benicio patted his son on the back. "You should consider becoming a chef," he teased.

Bruno laughed easily. "You know, you're not the first person to suggest that. I'll think about it."

"It's good to have you home. I know I've said it before, but I have to say it again. I hope you stay for a while." Rose hugged him.

Bruno squeezed her close. "I plan to. Have a good night, you two. You're sure you don't want to stay in the guest rooms?"

Benicio understood his concern. The drive to Rose's home would take over an hour. "I'll get her home in one piece."

"Okay, drive safely," Bruno said.

The three walked to the door, and Bruno waved on their way to the car.

Benicio opened the passenger door and Rose slipped in. After he strapped on his seatbelt, he started down the long driveway toward the street.

"Where are your glasses? I do not want to risk my safety because of your vanity," Rose said.

He tossed her an annoyed look, but in the darkness of the car, she simply stared back at him, uncaring.

"In the glove compartment," he muttered.

Rose shook her head. She handed them over, and he put them on his face.

"Happy now?"

"Yes."

He drove at a moderate rate. Mostly they didn't speak but, every now and again, chatted about their children and something funny their grandchildren had done, the music on the radio filling in the silence during the quiet moments.

The time passed quickly—too quickly. Before long, he pulled in front of the mansion he'd been forced to move out of almost four years ago.

Rose remained seated in the car. "I'm worried about Audra," she said.

"Why?"

"Something is wrong between her and Damon. Did you notice?"

"Not really. I *was* surprised to see him tonight."

Rose pursed her lips thoughtfully. "I got the impression his coming surprised Audra too." She sighed heavily. "I wish she would talk to me."

"She will when she's ready. If there is something wrong, maybe she's trying to sort things out on her own," Benicio said.

"I suppose."

Their children were all adults, but they alternated between the desire to fix their problems and the knowledge that they were quite capable of living their own lives.

"I won't keep you because it's already late. Thanks for the lift. Have a good night."

As Rose moved a hand to the handle, he said, "I'll walk you to the door."

"It's not necessary, Ben."

He ignored her and exited the vehicle, desperate to spend a few more moments with her. Every second counted.

They walked up the stairs to the double doors.

"Well, good night." She gazed up at him, holding the container of food in front of her, like a barrier between them.

"Did Sylvie say anything to you about the trip coming up?" Benicio asked.

A while ago, he learned Rose planned to join Sylvie Johnson and her husband Oscar Brooks on vacation in the Greek Islands. Oscar, his "friend," which he had great doubts about now, had also invited another man to keep Rose company on the trip. Benicio had been furious and demanded Oscar also allow him to attend.

"Yes, she did."

"So, you know I'm coming. Why haven't you said anything about it?"

Rose shrugged. "I planned to, eventually, if you didn't. So, how did you happen to be going on the same vacation I am?"

Despite broaching the topic, her question took him aback, and he stumbled around for an explanation. "I... well—"

"I'm surprised you could take two weeks off from your company."

Embarrassment burned his cheeks, but Benicio regrouped and shoved the glasses higher on his face. "You've always told me I work too much, so I decided to take your advice. A couple weeks off might be exactly what I need. So, I guess you and I will finally take that vacation you wanted."

"Yes—you, me, Sylvie, Oscar, and Oscar's friend. You're aware there will be a fifth person there?"

He bristled but hid his annoyance. "I'm aware. When Oscar invited me—"

"Oscar invited you on the trip?" She sounded surprised.

"He insisted I come. He... what is the word? Badgered me. I couldn't say no."

"Oh. You couldn't say no to him, but you never had any problem saying no to me." She spoke with quiet resignation, and sadness filled her eyes.

Benicio recognized his mistake and wanted to kick himself for the faux pas.

"Rosa, I..." He fumbled for an excuse but couldn't find one.

"It's okay. I'm glad you're taking time off. Your sons have followed your example for so long, maybe seeing you take a break will give them the incentive to cut back, as well. Money isn't everything, Ben."

The chiding, softly spoken words, cut through him. "I know that."

"Family is important too."

"I *know*. You know I know that, don't you?" He spoke with urgency, deeply concerned she could believe he prioritized dollars over family.

She tilted her head to the side. "Yes, I believe you do. Anyway, you know the drill. Text me when you get home, so I know you got home safely."

"*Sí, señora,*" he said, pretending to be annoyed.

She rolled her eyes, a reluctant smile coming to her face. Then she sobered, reaching up to touch his bearded cheek. His lungs deflated and his entire body relaxed as he leaned into her gentle touch.

"I wouldn't want anything to happen to you. Do as I say."

How many times had they had this exact conversation? He had lost count.

"Don't I always?"

If she answered truthfully, the answer was no. He did not always do as she asked, and he'd failed miserably in her most important ask. To this day, he couldn't understand how he managed to mess up his marriage and lose the love of his life. Stubborn, bull-headed, all because she wanted to spend more time with him. What an old fool he was.

"Good night, *mi amor.*" Holding her hand, he pressed his lips to her palm.

He felt her slight tremor before she pulled away. She averted her eyes, but not before he saw what he believed to be tears. Her sadness wrenched at his heart.

"Good night," she said in a thick voice, before going inside.

Benicio stood outside the door feeling lost, the same as every time he had to say goodbye to Rose. He did an excellent job hiding his feelings, but the past few years had been nothing short of agony. The trip to the Greek Islands might seem to be an odd decision. Why inject himself into a vacation his wife was taking? But he knew what he was doing and had a good reason.

He made his way down the steps to the car.

The trip to the Greek Islands represented the first step in his plan to win back his Rosa.

Chapter Ten

Damon pulled into the three-car garage and cut the headlights. He'd had an unusually busy day. He didn't get a chance to hit the gym with the fellas this morning because of a meeting with staff to discuss his business holdings and a modeling offer from Calvin Klein. Then he took a trip across town to spend time at the Boys' Club before stopping by his financial advisor's office to review changes in stocks and other investments he wanted to make.

He ate a late lunch with an old teammate from the Atlanta Braves and sat through meetings most of the afternoon. He ate dinner alone, deciding not to make the trip home and then have to go back downtown for after-dinner drinks with potential business partners.

When he retired a few years ago, he thought for sure he'd miss baseball, and at first, he did. But making deals became an exciting replacement—albeit a different type of excitement. The negotiations, the risk-taking, the planning involved—all made adrenaline spike in his blood.

He wished he'd been able to come home for dinner though. Audra's rich-flavored comfort foods had roped him in from the beginning and, during his ball-playing days, had gotten him in trouble with his nutritionist on more than one occasion. His biological mother hadn't been the best cook growing up, and most of the women he came in contact with didn't give a shit about that kind of stuff. When he met Audra and tasted her hand in the kitchen, he was low-hanging fruit. Easy pickings.

In so many ways, she'd been the kind of woman he hadn't consciously been looking for. Kind, nurturing, and protective of her family. He paid attention to the way she talked about her daughter, and when she finally let him meet Kerilyn and he saw the affectionate and loving way she treated the little girl, he knew she was the kind of woman he could build a family with.

He climbed the stairs to the second floor and peeked in on his children and then headed to the bedroom at the end of the hallway. Ever since he started sleeping in here more often, he brought in some of his clothes. He prepared for the following day by setting out pants and a shirt, something Audra used to do for him. So much had changed in their marriage, the most drastic changes taking place in the last six months when they stopped having sex altogether. They went from sending funny memes to each other over the course of the day to never cracking a smile when the other person entered the room.

What he missed most of all was how she soothed him. Being around her—holding her hand or simply snuggling together on the couch always brought him peace no matter what demons disrupted his day. Over time, she slipped further away, and he hated that he continued to need her so much. Even more, he hated the feeling of being... unwanted. He'd been there before with parents who should have never had a kid. The pain of rejection could be downright debilitating.

With a heavy sigh, he searched the top drawer of the dresser but couldn't find any socks. Was he out? He went into the laundry room but didn't see any in there. He checked the dryer. Nada.

Annoyed, he stalked down the hall to the master bedroom and knocked on the door. The irony of knocking on a door he used to walk through freely was not lost on him. That's how far their marriage had deteriorated.

He pressed an ear to the door, but no sound came from inside.

He knocked again and waited. Light filtered under the door, so Audra probably wasn't sleeping despite the late hour.

Turning the knob, he poked his head inside. "Audra?"

No sign of her. She must be in the bathroom or somewhere else in the house.

He crossed the floor and went into his walk-in closet on the other side of the California king bed. As he exited the closet with the socks in hand, Audra stepped out of the bathroom wrapped in a white towel and her hair piled on top of her head.

They both froze, albeit for different reasons. Her face held surprise. For Damon, the sight of his wife's smooth, dark-brown skin looking soft and dewy from being freshly washed robbed his lungs of air.

His shapely and curvaceous wife, with thick thighs and an ass plush enough to absorb his thrusts, had to be naked under that towel.

Damon recovered first. "Came to get some socks."

"Oh." Her eyes dipped to the socks in his hands. "So, you have everything you need?"

Her voice vibrated inside him and shot hot blood to his loins.

Nah, he didn't have everything he needed. Particularly

now, with his body reacting to the vision of her deliciously sexy curves in the white towel. He knew the pleasures of her body and couldn't help the response of *his* body—tightening skin, shorter breaths, hardening dick.

"Yeah," he said throatily.

He marched toward the door before he did something he regretted, like yank off the towel, lift her against the wall, and plunge his body as deep into hers as he possibly could. She'd probably slap the hell out of him for touching her after so long.

"You're sleeping in the guest room?"

She asked that question because she was wide awake, so the lame excuse of not wanting to disturb her wouldn't make sense tonight.

"Yeah, I'll probably go downstairs and watch television for a bit, so..."

"I see."

Neither moved, eyes latched on to each other, knowing he was lying.

"Good night." Damon turned toward the door.

"You should probably move all your things into the guest room, don't you think?"

She spoke quietly, but he heard every word, and they grated like nails on a chalkboard. The skin on the back of his neck prickled, and Damon slowly turned to face her.

Such a drastic step would be so... final. Capitulation. An admission that they were truly and finally done.

"Why?"

Audra shrugged her bare shoulders. "It would be more convenient, I guess."

"Convenient for who?" he asked, recognizing the antagonistic sound of his voice but unable to do anything to stop it.

"For you, of course."

Damon's fingers tightened around the socks. "And you, right?"

"I made a suggestion, Damon. I wasn't trying to pick a fight."

"That's quite a suggestion," he shot back.

"You seldom sleep in here anymore, so what's the point of keeping your clothes in the closet?"

He took a couple steps toward her. "I have a right to that closet."

"This should not be an argument about the closet."

"You brought up the closet."

She let out a short laugh and shook her head. "You know what, never mind. I was trying to be helpful, but everything I say is a problem." She stalked into her walk-in closet.

Damon followed. Riled up. Fuming. He hated losing his temper. He saw the loss of control as a sign of weakness, but no one frayed his nerves like his wife could, and he was still smarting from the conversation at Bruno's several days ago.

"Why don't you say it, Audra?"

She stopped rummaging in a drawer. "Say what?"

Her indifferent tone fueled his annoyance.

"Say what you been wanting to say for months. Say what's been on the tip of your tongue. In addition to not wanting me at Bruno's the other night, you don't want me around here anymore, either."

"*None* of that is true. I already told you that it surprised me when you showed up at Bruno's."

"Say it."

"I don't know what you want me to say," Audra pushed the words through clenched teeth.

She brushed past him with a nightgown in her hands, a filmy piece of cloth that made his balls ache. She was his wife.

His fucking wife, and he couldn't touch her. For months, he hadn't held the heft of her breasts or enjoyed the way her nipples pebbled against his palms when aroused. Couldn't remember the last time he'd drowned in the scent between her legs or filled his hands with her hips and ass.

Damon followed. She knew exactly what he wanted her to say. "You're a liar," he said, keeping his voice even.

She swung to face him, anger flashing in her eyes. "*You're* a liar. I am not."

"Nah, you are. You want to pretend to your family that everything is okay, when you know good and well nothing —*nothing* about this marriage is the way it should be."

"*I'm* pretending? After months of missing family events, you showed up like you hadn't purposely been skipping our dinners and get-togethers. Where were you during those periods, huh?"

He only bothered to go because he let Zack's comment about her screwing someone else get in his head. Her indifference to his attendance rubbed him the wrong way, and he became paranoid. With the knowledge that the Connor-Santanas sometimes invited guests to their get-togethers—actors, businessmen, friends of the family—he couldn't help but wonder if there was someone hanging around that she had become attracted to.

"Like you care where I am or what I do," he said with a bitter laugh.

"Why should I? You don't tell me where you go or what you're doing. You could be fucking another woman for all I know."

"I am *not* cheating on you."

"So you say."

"It's the truth!"

She laughed shrilly. "My husband sleeps in the room down

the hall and sometimes stays out late, and I don't know where he is. Yes, I must be mistaken about whatever my assumptions are."

He shook his head. "You know what, talking to you is a waste of time."

"I'm surprised you've said this much. Usually I do all the talking, and you mumble something incoherent and then we're done."

The stinging retort lashed his skin and laid bare his flaw.

"What would you prefer? You want a man who growls and yells and stomps around all the time? That's what you prefer?"

"I prefer a man who talks. Who tells me what he's *feeling*, Damon. Do you have feelings?"

"That's what you want?" Damon nodded slowly, at the end of his rope. Horny, mad, and helpless in the face of this inexplicable anger between them. "Okay, here goes. I'm miserable, and I'm sick of this bullshit marriage. I'm sick of pretending everything is okay when it's not. I hate coming home because I don't know what to say to you anymore. I can't make you happy, and I'm sure as hell not happy. So there, that's me laying everything out there and sharing my *feelings*, like you wanted me to do. Happy now?"

Hurt filled her eyes, and Damon immediately regretted the words. He wanted to suck them back or rewind time and start over. He'd gone too far and opened his mouth to say as much, but she spoke first.

"I want a divorce."

The words landed in the room with grenade-like force and sliced through him like pieces of shrapnel. Damon blinked and took a step back. Shocked. Confused. Disoriented. His heart thundered in his chest. He'd anticipated the end of their marriage, yet to actually hear the words caused him unbelievable pain—way more than any sports injury or when his father's fists battered his body.

"What did you say?" He pushed the words past numb lips.

Audra dropped her gaze for a moment and took a deep breath. When she looked at him again, her eyes were clear, her face resolute. "I want a divorce. You want a divorce. *We* want a divorce. We can't continue living like this, like—like strangers. And I don't want our children to see us behave like enemies."

The agony of defeat weighed heavy on his shoulders.

"It's for the best," she added.

The best for who? Damon thought. Her, clearly. She wanted to be free of him. His mind couldn't compute the drastic change in the past few seconds.

"You want to end our marriage," he said.

"You said you're not happy, so why are we doing this? Why torture each other?"

In sports, he knew what to do to improve his game. Study the opposition and train harder. What was the remedy for a failing marriage? Giving up couldn't be the only option.

"Fine. But you're not keeping me from my kids."

Her eyes widened. "I would never do that," she said, sounding appalled that he had accused her of something so heinous.

"Damn right."

He kept his voice low but clear. For him, raised voices meant emotions out of control. Out of control meant incoming strikes.

"What do we do now?" Audra asked in a quiet voice.

He let out a short laugh. For months, he and Audra had treated each other with deft gloves and for the most part, kept their distance even when in the same room. That would all come to an end now. They had finally said the unthinkable.

"Do whatever you want. I don't give a shit anymore."

Damon stalked across the carpet and swung the door open and walked out.

"Wonderful!" she screamed behind him. "I don't give a shit either!"

Then he heard the door slam shut.

Chapter Eleven

Audra was shaking. They had been leading up to a blow out for months. Nonetheless, the argument felt surreal.

I want a divorce.

She stared at the closed door, wanting to take back the words. Unfortunately, they were already out there because of fear. His words had shocked and frightened her. Before he bailed on her, she bailed on him.

Of course, he seemed undaunted by the idea of them splitting apart. Two seconds after telling him she wanted a divorce, he made a demand about the kids. He didn't give a crap about her anymore. Why should he? Women propositioned him all the time because of his celebrity status, and her husband was fine as hell. If he wasn't already sleeping with another woman, he could have one by the end of the week without trying. Sooner if he put forth some effort.

She dressed, slipping on her nightgown and then pacing the room like a restless, caged tigress. He barged into *her* bedroom—the master bedroom basically belonged to her now—and picked a fight. Then he left because *he* was done talking.

She used to think of him as the strong, silent type and think that character trait was sexy. Now she hated it with a passion.

She allowed emotion to rule her thoughts and actions while he remained cool in the most stressful situations. It drove her crazy. Arguing with him was like arguing with a wall. She rarely got a rise out of him and understood the reason was a combination of factors. Living with a tyrannical father and playing professional baseball, where the strain of being under a microscope meant having to perform in front of millions to prove your worth. Both had chiseled his character into emotionless calm.

Mr. Calm and Cool, she thought angrily.

Well, she didn't care if he was finished. *She* was not done talking.

Audra pulled on her robe and strode down the hallway to the guest room. She knocked on the door, and Damon immediately yanked it open from the other side, as if he'd been waiting for her.

Audra took in a sharp breath. He'd changed into pajama bottoms and no shirt. She couldn't remember the last time she'd seen her husband's bare chest. How pathetic.

Her eyes roamed over the words on his left pec.

Love is patient. Love is kind.

1 Corinthians 13:4

She licked her dry lips, trying to ignore the throb that emerged between her thighs.

"What are you doing here, Audra?"

He asked the question with a quirked brow, as if he already knew the answer. He knew she couldn't let things go. Their arguments dragged on because she needed to speak her mind and let out all her thoughts, while he eventually shut down and walked away, making her feel like an irrational shrew.

Audra pushed her way inside the room and swung to face him. "We need to talk."

Damon closed the door and folded his arms across his chest. She wished he hadn't done that. It only served to make his biceps more prominent.

"You don't want to talk. You want to fight."

"And you don't?"

"*I* want to go to sleep," he said.

"Not before I say my piece. Since we're in agreement about getting a divorce, we need to get a few things settled."

He let out a bitter laugh. "My, my, don't you move fast. But let's be real, you don't want to get shit settled. You want to argue some more, and I'm not in the mood."

"Less than ten minutes ago we agreed to divorce. What am I supposed to do, climb under the covers and go to sleep as if nothing happened?" Audra snapped.

"That's what I plan to do," Damon said in a dry tone.

"We need to discuss next steps."

"And what exactly do you think the next steps should be?" He rested his hands on his hips and waited for her response.

"I don't know, Damon. I've never gone through a divorce before!" she yelled.

He maintained a calm demeanor. "You're the one who mentioned divorce. Don't tell me you haven't been thinking about it. You probably have a lawyer picked out already."

"I do not, but that is something I will be doing very soon."

She watched him amble over to the window and yank the curtain closed.

"We should talk about living arrangements," Audra said.

His jaw tightened. "What about our living arrangements?"

Audra straightened her back. "We basically don't share the

same room anymore, so—so I think we should make that permanent. This is now your bedroom, but we need to go further. We should separate for a while, give each other space —to think. To work out how to proceed next. Our emotions are high."

"You mean your emotions."

"Fine! My emotions. We need to separate for our own peace of mind, as well as for the kids."

He nodded. "I hear you. I hear everything you're saying, and what you said makes sense. When are you moving out?"

She blinked. Had she heard him correctly? "What do you mean when am I moving out? When we separate—"

"You're moving out." He spoke in a deadpan voice.

"Damon, this isn't funny."

"I'm not being funny. You brought it up, so I figured you'd be the one to move out. Oh, you thought it would be me leaving our kids?"

"Are you insane!" Audra yelled. "I am their mother."

"And I'm their father. I am not. Going to be separated. From my kids. I'm raising them in the house I bought to raise them in. If you think I'm moving out... *fuck that.*"

Audra stared at him, speechless.

He nodded. "You didn't see that coming, did you, when you brought up your little solution. Doesn't seem like such a great idea anymore, does it? I'm not leaving my kids, Audra. I don't want to be apart from them anymore than you do, so I guess we're stuck for the moment. Unless you plan to move out?" He arched an eyebrow.

"We're talking about divorce. There's no way we can continue to live under the same roof and function like a normal family."

"Then move out. Go stay with your mother while you figure things out. She's got plenty of space and would be happy to have you. Maybe not under these specific circumstances, but she won't turn you away."

"You can't separate a mother from her children."

"But you can a father?" He tilted his head to the side. "You know how much being a father means to me, and you don't have any qualms about asking me to leave my kids behind."

A sense of guilt washed over her. Damon was a fierce and loving father, perhaps more so because he wanted to provide the security and love his own father had never offered.

"I know you love the kids."

"Then how can you ask me to move?"

"At some point—"

"When we get to that point, we'll deal with it. I'm not leaving, Audra."

"Then I'll take them," she blurted, watching with satisfaction as his eyes widened a fraction. "Like you said, my mother has plenty of room at her house. I'll take the kids and move in with her."

Despite Damon remaining very still, she sensed the undercurrent of fury.

"Over my dead body."

With those words, he'd thrown down the gauntlet. He would not leave, and he would not allow her to take the children.

A noise outside the door caught Audra's attention. "What's that?"

"What's what?" Damon asked.

She rushed across the carpet and pulled open the door. Her heart dropped to her feet when she saw Tracy sitting curled against the wall, arms wrapped around her knees, head bent. Her stuffed rabbit lay on the floor beside her, and she was crying.

"Baby." Audra dropped to her haunches. "What are you doing up?"

"I heard you and Daddy." Her little voice quivered. She peered around Audra to look up at her father, who had come to stand behind Audra.

"We were having a conversation and got a little loud. Did we wake you?" Audra brushed away the tears on her cheeks with the back of her hand.

Tracy nodded, sniffling.

"I'm sorry. Next time we'll have to be quieter." Audra stood and lifted her daughter in her arms. Tracy rested her head on her shoulder.

"Sorry about that, baby. Mommy and Daddy got a little excited during our conversation," Damon said, keeping his eyes on Audra.

"Daddy, are you going to leave us?" Tracy asked.

"No, I'm not going anywhere." Damon stroked the bonnet that protected her twists.

Though he spoke in a soothing voice to their daughter, Audra didn't miss the underlying steeliness in his voice. He picked up the blue rabbit and handed it to Tracy, who clutched the toy like a lifeline.

"I guess we'll have to finish talking tomorrow," Damon said.

"I guess so." Holding tight to Tracy, Audra left him in the doorway.

She walked down the hallway on rubbery legs that barely carried her. When she laid Tracy in the bed and tucked her under the sheets, her sleepy-eyed daughter stared up at her.

"Mommy, are you going to leave us?"

The question tore at her conscience, breaking her heart and adding guilt to the jumble of emotions inside her.

"No, baby. Not at all. Everything is fine, okay?" Audra bit her lip to keep it from trembling. She kissed Tracy on the forehead and wiped away the remnants of tears on her round cheeks. "Get some sleep, so you'll be well rested for camp in the morning."

"Okay." Hugging the rabbit, Tracy turned on her side.

Audra remained seated on the bed until she fell asleep. Listening to Tracy's even breathing and the even breathing of her son across the room, she blinked back tears.

At this point, the children were the only thing holding her marriage together. Without them, she and Damon might have gone their separate ways already.

She left the room, and when she reached the master bedroom, she peered down the hall. The light in the guest bedroom where Damon slept was out.

She missed having his love and attention. Missed having him lie next to her at night and waking up to him in the morning. Missed his "bad" habit of rolling over in the middle of the night and pulling her close, as if to make sure she was there. Almost as much as she missed his presence as her husband, she would miss the way he loved their children.

Then she had a panic-inducing premonition. If his comments were any indication, he would fight her for custody. He might be done with her and their marriage, but he wouldn't give up the kids without a fight.

Her lips firmed.

Well, neither would she.

Chapter Twelve

After several days of phone calls, Audra sat in the office of DeMarcus & Lyfe, divorce and family law attorneys, the first attorney whose office she had visited.

She hadn't experienced a connection with the others, but this particular law firm gave her the impression of professionalism and friendliness at the same time. They had a great reputation and their customer service had been top notch. An associate returned her call right away and set up an in-person consultation upon hearing her circumstances.

She did not, however, like what she'd just heard. "What do you mean he doesn't have to leave?"

With blemish-free cocoa skin, black glasses, and her hair in a neat knot atop her head, Faydra DeMarcus had the polished air of competence Audra wanted in an attorney. A bulldog, from what she could tell, but her current answer to Audra's question didn't sound like bulldog behavior.

"It's his home too, and we can't force him to move without a legal order," Faydra explained. "Which he'll fight, if what you've told me so far is any indication. He has no intention of leaving the primary residence. With that in mind, do you really want to try to force him out when, in fact, he could turn the tables on you?"

"I'm their *mother*."

"I understand, but from what you've told me, he's a good father, isn't he?" Faydra flipped back one page on her notepad. "During the school year, he takes the children to school and picks them up most days. Sometimes he fixes breakfast on the weekends, spends quality time with your children by playing with them, going for bike rides and walks in the neighborhood—"

"Yes, yes, yes," Audra said irritably. She didn't want to cut Damon out of their children's lives, but she and he needed space from each other.

"Those are your words, not mine," Faydra said gently. "Unless you can provide evidence that he's not a good father. Has there been any abuse or neglect you haven't told me about?"

Audra shook her head. "No, he's a great father. He'd rather die than hurt our kids."

In fact, she was the disciplinarian, and threatening the kids that she'd tell their father about their bad behavior didn't strike fear in them. Instead, it made them ashamed because they didn't want to disappoint him.

"That's a good thing, you know."

"I know. But..." Audra let out a frustrated breath. "What do I do? Don't we have to be legally separated before I can get a divorce?"

"The good news is, in Georgia you can be legally separated even if you remain in the same house. When did you discuss him permanently moving to the guest bedroom?"

"Three days ago."

"A thirty-day separation is the minimum recommended period, and the clock started then. You're no longer intimate?"

Audra's cheeks burned. "No," she said in a low voice. "We haven't done anything in months."

"Good. Keep it that way. Having sex while separated could complicate the divorce proceedings."

"Trust me, that won't be an issue." Damon no longer reached for her, and they did a very good job of avoiding touching.

She'd almost forgotten the pleasure of his hands on her bare skin and the tug of his mouth on her nipples. *Almost.* She wished she could. Then the intense longing would go away.

He used to hold her hand all the time and rub her butt if he came into the kitchen and she stood at the stove. Sometimes he annoyed the hell out of her because she'd be busy, and here he'd come, rubbing or squeezing her butt. She missed those moments. They showed he wanted her. The absence of his touch devastated her more than she could have ever imagined.

"I know the process seems overwhelming at the moment, but remember you're in the beginning stages. A lot has to be worked out. Especially in a case like yours because you're a very wealthy couple. Marital assets have to be divided, there's spousal support to consider, and then of course, there's the issue of custody. Children complicate divorce."

"How long do you think the divorce could take?" Audra asked.

"If you're both agreeable on the terms, not long at all. A few months. If you're not, the process could drag on for a year or longer. In extreme cases, for years. But let's not get ahead of ourselves. I'd love to be your attorney if you'd let me."

Audra nodded, the weight of her decision robbing her of speech. This was truly the end for her and Damon. They were getting a divorce. Panic pressed the inner wall of her chest.

"I would like for you to represent me," Audra said, biting the inside of her trembling bottom lip.

"Good. Let me know as soon as you have the name of his attorney. I'll be in touch in the next day or two. I'll need a copy of your prenup. I'll also have questions I need you to answer and paperwork to fill out. As soon as you return everything to me, I'll get you set up in the system so we can get started. The documents will also explain about our retainer and the discovery phase, where we gather information on both sides." Her eyes softened and she sat forward, reaching a hand across the desk.

Audra placed her hand in Faydra's and felt a reassuring squeeze.

"Let me do the worrying for you," Faydra said. "Keep your chin up and have a positive attitude for your teenager and little ones. Okay?"

Audra nodded, grateful for the words of encouragement. "Okay. Thanks."

Minutes later, she sat in her car in the parking garage and cried—face pressed into her open palms with the back of her hands resting on the steering wheel, shoulders slumped as gut-wrenching sobs racked her body.

She cried for a full thirty minutes.

* * *

"I can't believe I'm getting a divorce, Simon," Damon said.

He rolled his friend's stress ball around in his hand as he scanned the Atlanta cityscape. He had come to Simon's office seeking a referral for a divorce attorney, but he also needed him as a friend. He hadn't slept much since the argument with Audra, lack of sleep evident in his bleary eyes and haggard appearance.

"I'm sorry you've reached this point, but divorce doesn't have to be acrimonious. Of course, with assets like yours... I hope you have an ironclad prenup."

Damon turned away from the window. "Right now, I don't care about all that. I'm worried about my kids. I don't want to be limited to spending holidays and weekends with them. I never envisioned myself being a part-time father. You know the shitty upbringing I had before I was adopted. I always wanted to be involved in my children's lives, but now..."

He recalled the early days of life with two little ones. Baby-proofing the house, overreacting and putting a mirror under their noses in the middle of the night to make sure they were breathing, making silly faces over and over again to hear their cute baby laughs.

They were older now but no less enjoyable. He couldn't fathom not waking up under the same roof with his children, seeing them off to school, taking Junior for his haircuts and teaching him and Tracy how to drive the same way he'd done his oldest.

"Just because she's their mother doesn't mean she'll get custody," Simon pointed out. "Courts are different now. Fathers have more rights than ever. They share custody and, in some cases, get full custody. Though this isn't my area of law expertise, from what I understand, you're technically already separated now that you're officially sleeping in separate bedrooms. There's no law that says you have to live separately from each other."

"You think we should continue living together?"

Simon shrugged. "It's been done before, but you can't muddy the waters by sleeping together again."

Damon crossed the carpeted floor and placed the ball on the desk. "That won't happen. It's been awhile."

"How long?"

"A long time," Damon said, too embarrassed to admit how long he and Audra hadn't made love.

Her body used to be very responsive to his. With the slightest swipe of his tongue, her nipple would stiffen in his mouth. She no longer enjoyed sex with him and had started simply going through the motions. Was she even attracted to him anymore?

"You think she's seeing anyone?" Simon asked carefully.

"What?" Damon asked sharply.

"It happens."

"I don't want to think about that."

Granted, things between them weren't great, but any man who thought he could come between him and his wife would have hell to pay.

"What about you? Are you seeing anyone? I only ask because dirt like that could affect the terms of the divorce."

"I told you at the gym, there's no one else but Audra." She was his life. There wasn't a piece of ass—natural or otherwise—worth losing his life over.

"Okay, so what do you want to do?"

Damon sighed. "I'm upset, but I don't want to lose my wife and family, man."

He hadn't fully processed what losing them meant because he couldn't face that kind of pain and upheaval.

"Have you tried counseling?"

Damon snorted as he dropped into the chair across from his friend. "Do I look like the kind of person who'd pay a shrink to give him advice? I don't believe in that. Those people take your money and nothing good ever happens. There are folks in therapy for years."

"Couples therapy is different. Think of it as a tune up for your marriage."

Damon frowned. "Sounds like you're talking from experience."

Color tinged his friend's cheeks. "I am. I wasn't exactly excited about spilling my guts about my innermost thoughts and feelings to a stranger, but Dr. Lewis is pretty good."

"What makes him so good?"

"She."

"Oh great, a female therapist. I bet she blamed you for everything, right?"

Simon laughed. "Not at all. She forced us to examine our relationship in a new way. I'm telling you, it worked. She says marriages are made up of rainy days and sunny days. The key to a lasting marriage is not to let the rain drench you. The key is to huddle *together* under the umbrella until the storm clouds past. Then you can enjoy the sunny days again."

"Sounds like mumbo jumbo to me."

"She saves marriages and promises results in as little as six weeks."

That caught his attention. "No way."

"Didn't take that long for me and Elsa," Simon continued in an earnest voice. "We went every week for five weeks and then cut back to every two weeks. Then we didn't need to go at all. I'm telling you, she's good. Do you have any feelings left for your wife?"

"Yes."

Not only did he have feelings for her, he loved her like no one else. He craved her. Longed to touch her. The only reason he'd cut back on sleeping in their bedroom was to avoid the torture of lying next to her every night. Despite not sleeping together, he occasionally woke up in the middle of the night, blindly reaching across the bed to find only cool sheets. Then he'd have to lay there, his chest hurting, knowing his wife slept soundly down the hall without him.

"If that's the case, then take this card." Simon handed him a silver card with black letters. "If Audra is interested in working things out, give Dr. Lewis a call. I think she can help."

Damon didn't believe in therapy. His adoptive parents had wanted him to see a shrink to help him deal with the trauma of his past, but he knew talking didn't work. His father had gone to therapy for his abusive behavior. He'd also taken anger management classes. None of that kept him from putting his hands on Damon and his mother.

But the alternative—giving up on his marriage—didn't seem like much of an option at all.

"Thanks." He tucked the card into his wallet.

He didn't believe in therapy, but Audra did. If therapy could fix his relationship and keep his family together, then he'd suffer through the sessions and accept whatever hokey advice Dr. Lewis threw their way.

Chapter Thirteen

Kerilyn was unusually quiet at breakfast. Audra noticed she'd been that way for several days, but when she tried to talk to her daughter, she denied anything was wrong.

The little ones talked nonstop to each other like normal. Tracy had either forgotten what happened Monday night, or she didn't deem the incident worthy of further reflection. As a bonus, Audra didn't have any trouble out of her as she happily ate a bowl of cereal, feet swinging under the table, while the other two enjoyed waffles and eggs.

Now that she'd talked to an attorney, Audra dreaded seeing Damon. She almost felt... guilty. As if she'd done something wrong. He didn't come into the kitchen, though. Instead, he called for Kerilyn, Tracy, and Junior from the front door.

At the sound of his commanding voice, all three scrambled from the table, shouting their goodbyes on the way out. She didn't know if he ever turned an eye to her because she never looked through the French doors at him. She kept wiping the counters as if they were covered in three inches of dirt.

After they all left, she stopped her manic cleaning. Standing in the middle of the kitchen, she blinked back the urge to cry. She had built a fantasy around their life and family, which was shattered beyond repair.

Resting her hands on the counter, she bent her head. Her heart ached with misery and regret. She wanted to scream, but the sound stayed trapped in her throat.

Breathe. You got this, she told herself.

* * *

Damon eased the car to a stop outside the Alliance for Arts & Science, a camp that kept Junior and Tracy busy all day. He nodded at one of the dads escorting his daughter to the front door. Boys and girls ran around, taking advantage of the period before classes started. A facilitator watched the youngsters swinging and sliding on the playground, while the head of the program and one of the teachers kept their eyes on the children at the front of the building and made sure the car line kept moving.

"All right, guys, see you later. Have a good day."

"Bye, Daddy! Bye, Keri!" The younger two hopped out the back and ran toward the front door.

Damon watched them go inside before he pulled out of the lot, on the way to the next stop.

So far, Kerilyn seemed to enjoy the work she did for her uncle, but Ethan had told her if she wanted to do something else, he'd find a spot for her in a different department.

They drove toward the company in silence for a while before Damon glanced at Kerilyn. She'd been oddly quiet all week.

"You okay, Keri?"

She nodded. "I'm fine."

"You sure?"

She gazed out the side window. "Yeah." Her voice sounded dull and listless.

He weaved between cars. "You know you can talk to me, right?"

She swallowed but didn't look at him. "I know." She whispered the words, as if she had a hard time saying them.

Damon finally pulled in front of the building, the seat of Ethan's global real estate empire.

"All right, I'll see you later."

"Kayleigh wants to hang out at the mall. Is it okay if she picks me up from work?" Kerilyn asked.

"Did you tell your mom? You know she doesn't like you driving with Kayleigh. She's only had her license for a couple of months."

"Mom never lets me do anything," Kerilyn said in a tired voice.

"Because she doesn't—"

"I know, because she doesn't want me to make the same mistakes she did. But the mall isn't a dangerous place, and Kayleigh's careful." Her eyes pleaded with him.

Damon sighed. "All right. But send your mom a text so she knows where you are and with who, and let her know I gave you permission."

"I will." Head bowed, she didn't move.

"Was there something else?" Damon asked gently.

"Can I talk to you?" Kerilyn asked tentatively, keeping her head bent.

Something must be seriously wrong. His stomach rolled with a sense of dread.

"Of course."

Kerilyn swallowed hard. "I heard you and Mom Monday night," she said quietly.

Damon released a quiet sigh. "You should have been asleep."

"I wasn't."

Clearly. Yelling and slamming doors certainly didn't help.

"I'm sorry you had to hear that."

"So, you're getting a divorce?"

She finally lifted her gaze. The sadness in her eyes raked his heart, but he needed to be honest. No benefit came from trying to candy coat the situation.

"Yes, that's what we decided. It's been coming for a while."

Kerilyn nodded her acknowledgment. "I figured, since you're always sleeping in the guest room," she said in a low voice.

Damon didn't know how much people outside of the house recognized the rift between him and Audra, but he wasn't surprised Kerilyn came to that conclusion. Hard not to, when your parents slept in separate bedrooms and some nights your father came home at odd hours.

"I guess you're going to move out?" Kerilyn asked.

Hell no, he wanted to yell. "I haven't thought that far ahead. Getting divorced was a split-second decision."

"So maybe you won't get a divorce." Her voice and eyes became hopeful.

Damon rubbed the back of his neck. "I don't know, Keri. Like I said, this has been coming for a while. Your mom and I..."

"You don't love each other anymore," she finished glumly.

The words cut deep. He knew how he felt, but thinking Audra had fallen out of love with him hit hard, like punches to the solar plexus.

He cleared his throat. "Marriage is complicated and takes a

lot of work and energy. Both parties have to want to make it work."

"If you and Mom split up, what does that mean—for us?"

"What do you mean?" Damon asked, trying to get to the root of her concern.

She gnawed on her lip, uncertainty in her eyes. "Will you still be my dad?" she asked in a low, trembling voice.

"Of course. That won't change."

Goddammit. The fallout from the divorce had already started, and the front of a commercial building wasn't the best place to have this conversation. Damon checked the rearview mirror and eased away from the entrance. He pulled into a lot across the street and turned off the SUV's engine. Bracing his hand on top of his daughter's seat, he leaned toward her.

"Look at me." She reluctantly lifted her eyes. "The divorce doesn't change anything between us. You're not mine by blood, but you're mine in here." He tapped the spot over his heart.

He entered her life when she was six years old. Her biological father was not much of a father then, and his role had diminished over the years as his band grew in popularity. Damon gladly took his place and lovingly referred to Kerilyn as his daughter from the start of the marriage. One of the most emotional days in his life occurred the first time she tentatively, shyly called him *Dad*.

"You're not my real dad," Kerilyn said.

"I *am* your real dad. Just because I'm not your biological father doesn't mean I'm not. That's not what makes a dad. I've raised you, and I love you. You're mine."

Doubt continued to register in her expression. "Kayleigh's stepmom left after her parents divorced, and now she's sad all the time because she doesn't have a mom anymore."

He'd heard about their divorce. They supposedly had an

amicable split, but there were whispers of infidelity—mainly that Kayleigh's stepmother had an affair with someone at their church.

"I can't speak to their situation, only ours. I'll always be in your life, like I'll always be in Junior's and Tracy's. You're no different. Even when you're sick of me, I'll still be your dad."

A faint smile touched the corners of her lips. Then she frowned. He waited as she sorted through her thoughts.

"Why can't you and Mom work things out? Is your relationship really that bad?"

"Things happen, sweetheart. In our case, we basically grew apart."

"Can't you grow back together?" she asked with a hitch in her voice.

Hearing her pain brought home how devastating his breakup with Audra would be for the kids.

"Doesn't work like that," he said. "But me and your mom splitting up doesn't change anything else."

"*Everything* will change. We won't celebrate holidays together anymore, and we'll have to live separate from each other. We'll see mom every day but not you."

Damon resolved then and there to be a constant presence in their lives, no matter what the future held. "Look, we're getting ahead of ourselves, okay? For now, we don't have to think about visitation and all that, but know I'll make every effort to see the three of you often. Not only on weekends. Not only on holidays. I'm always going to be in your life," he promised.

"I hope the two of you can work things out."

So did Damon. "Don't worry about what's going on with your mom and me right now. Those are grown up problems, and that's for me and her to work through. Whatever we decide, we will always put you and your brother and sister first.

You're always our priority. We'll do our best to make sure you're not negatively impacted—well, too much. But we haven't made any final decisions yet, so we need time to sort through all of that, okay? And do me a favor, don't mention any of this to your brother and sister yet."

"I won't."

"Good. You have any more questions for me?"

She shook her head.

"All right. You better go before you're late."

"See you later."

Kerilyn pushed open the door, but before she could hop out the vehicle, Damon grabbed her arm.

"Love you, Little Bit," he said.

He wanted her to have complete confidence that he wouldn't leave her simply because he and her mother were splitting up. He used the nickname he had given her when they first met, which she grew to hate as she grew taller than her mother.

Instead of rolling her eyes like she used to, her face brightened, and she said what she used to. "I'm not little."

Damon smiled.

Kerilyn climbed out the car and paused. "Love you—Dad."

She closed the door and rushed toward the entrance of the building. He watched her meet up with another employee on the way, and the two of them walked inside together.

Alone again, the smile fell off Damon's face. A giant hole had already opened in his heart when he considered how life would change when he and Audra divorced. Which week days and holidays would he be allotted to have time with his children? Thinking about the ramifications of his family being torn apart made him want to slam his fist into a wall.

The thought of his children suffering was completely unacceptable. He couldn't sit back and not take steps to prevent their pain.

He pulled out his wallet and removed the silver card Simon had given him the day before. He would no longer delay broaching the topic of counseling with Audra. They needed to talk right away.

Chapter Fourteen

Audra had a full morning. After she washed the dishes and cleaned up the kitchen, the two women from the cleaning service arrived.

"Hi Lola, hi Wendy," she greeted, letting them into the house with their supplies.

"Hello, Mrs. Foster."

Audra directed the women to the areas she wanted them to focus on. While they cleaned and dusted, the grocery delivery arrived, and she unpacked the items, putting everything away in the refrigerator and pantry.

When the maids left, she ate a late lunch and then went into the she shed to work on her blog. She punched in the code on the door panel and entered the workspace for Plush, her lifestyle website.

Because Damon recognized her passion for fine goods and eye for style, he encouraged her to turn the website into a business. Plush took off when she joined Instagram, upon the advice of her younger sister, Monica. When Damon saw her success, he offered to build her own space. He liked working with his hands and jumped at the chance to put together items around the house. A bookcase for her novels, shelving to display Tracy's dolls, and this structure.

At first, she believed an office was too much, but now she enjoyed having a separate space to call her own. The exterior was made of cedar wood and topped by a sloped black roof. Inside appeared roomy because of the nine-foot ceiling and how plenty of light entered the space from the glass doors and the window on one side. She had a black accent wall and brightened the rest of the space with a wood desk, white chair, and an off-white rug anchored by a yellow sofa she found for a steal at an estate sale. Potted plants and a floor lamp enhanced the décor and made the office a comfortable escape from the rest of the house.

Damon spent a day and a half assembling the shed. He would have finished sooner if he hadn't received "help" from Junior. At one point, she took them each a glass of water, and when her eyes met Damon's, she saw the amusement in his. Because he *knew*. Watching him work turned her on. She'd never been more aroused than when she watched his muscular body drenched in sweat as he pounded nails and hauled wood. Not even when she watched him round the bases of the baseball diamond, a sexy performance in and of itself.

No doubt, she liked to see her man work.

Audra turned on the computer and took her notebook from the middle shelf of three built above the desk. She planned to review her notes and draft a few posts for her blog, but set aside her plans when she saw the email from Faydra.

Apprehension burned her chest like acid. With trembling fingers, she double tapped the message and read the instructions on how to log into the firm's system and what to do with the attached forms. Faydra had listed everything she needed to do to start the divorce proceedings, but Audra sat frozen. The finality of the next steps kept her immobile.

A knock on the glass door shook her from her stupor.

With a quick glance over her shoulder, she saw Damon standing outside and immediately tensed.

"Come in," she said.

He slid open the door and stepped inside, dominating the small space in a long-sleeved cotton shirt with the sleeves pushed up to reveal sinewy forearms. The only three buttons were undone to expose his strong throat and the hint of hair on his chest. Gray pants hugged his thighs and hips like a lover's embrace, making her focus on his face to avoid the claw of need that threatened to overtake her.

Now that she'd been told she could jeopardize the divorce if they slept together, she was more aware of him. As if someone dangled a carrot in front of her.

"We need to talk," Damon said in a grave voice.

Audra closed the laptop cover. "Okay," she said, watching him warily.

He leaned against the wall beside her desk. "I've been thinking about the divorce and how it'll tear our family apart."

"If you—"

He lifted a hand. "Let me finish, Audra. You always complain that I don't talk enough, so let me get what I have to say off my chest and then you can speak."

She hated the chastising tone of his voice but clamped her mouth shut.

"Have you talked to an attorney?" Damon asked.

"Yes," Audra admitted reluctantly. "Have you?" The question caught in her throat and had to be forcibly pushed across her tongue.

"I went to Simon for a referral, but talking to him made me

think we should reconsider. If for no other reason, for the sake of the kids."

Audra dropped her gaze to hide the hurt his words caused. He wanted to stay together because of their children. Not because he loved her. Not because he regretted that their marriage had fallen apart years after they promised to be together until death.

"That's not a reason to stay together," she said.

"It's as good a reason as any. We have to figure out how to live in peace, for the sake of our children. Do you really want to shuttle them between two houses until they're grown?"

"I'm as concerned about their welfare as you are, but we're not staying together because of them. That's ridiculous."

A muscle in his jaw flexed. "You saw how upset Tracy was the other night."

"That's because she heard us arguing."

"Well, Keri also heard us arguing, and I had an interesting talk with her when I dropped her off at work." He recounted their conversation, and when he finished, waited for her response.

More guilt flooded her system. She hated this terrible situation so much.

"I don't want them to be hurt, but you and I... we're no longer happy."

"What if we could become happy again, like when we first got married?"

They'd gotten married because she was pregnant, and she'd been too embarrassed to face her family with another out-of-wedlock pregnancy. She'd only been with two men in her life and became pregnant by both of them. Damon had been anxious to tie the knot because he'd wanted to start a family.

When he retired a few years ago, much speculation swirled in the news. Some articles blamed Audra for the sudden announcement, but he left because that's what they had agreed to. She would stay home, they would live below their means, and he would invest most of his income, allowing him to retire early so he could be more involved in their children's lives. They had agreed on so many aspects of married life, but somehow everything went wrong.

"I don't know if we can get back to that," Audra said dully.

"We should try. Unless there's some reason you don't want to."

His voice hardened on the second sentence, and her head snapped up.

"What are you implying?"

"Are you seeing someone else?"

"*No.*"

"I see all those men flirting with you on your Instagram page."

"Those men are strangers being absolutely ridiculous."

"Do you like it?" he asked, watching her closely.

"I don't encourage them, Damon."

His jawline hardened. "That's not what I asked."

"You're being—"

"Answer the question."

She hopped to her feet. "Stop cutting me off! Anyone would be flattered when the opposite sex finds them attractive. Yes, their comments are great for my ego. *You* get attention all the time. When we go anywhere, people stare at you, and they want your autograph. Women approach you when they recognize who you are. Sometimes they flirt while I'm standing *right there.*"

He straightened from the wall. "Don't I handle those situations? I never let anyone disrespect you."

"No, you don't, but it doesn't change the fact that it happens. Over and over and over again. So yes, Damon. I'm flattered when men make comments on my Instagram page. I'm human. Where exactly are you going when you stay out late at night? You could be with another woman, for all I know."

"I already told you, I'm not," he said between clenched teeth.

"Why don't I believe that," Audra murmured.

"I don't see why you would doubt me."

"You stay out all hours of the night. For months, most nights you slept in one of the other rooms. What else am I supposed to think?" She paced over to the sofa, no longer comfortable standing so close with him towering over her.

"When I'm out, I'm either at the office or with the guys. Sometimes I go by the cigar bar and chill. I've never touched another woman since you and I have been married. That's the truth, whether you believe me or not."

She wanted to believe him, but so much had changed between them. If he could just reach for her one time, to show he still cared.

"We can't even have a simple conversation without us getting angry. How are we supposed to work through whatever is wrong in our marriage?" she asked.

So often when they talked, their words became weapons, and they tossed them at each other like battle axes. Perhaps because arguing was easier than getting to the root of the problem.

"We don't have to figure out our problems alone. Simon gave me the name of a marriage therapist. He said she helped him and Elsa when they went through a difficult period in their marriage. Supposedly, if we give her six weeks, she can... fix whatever is wrong with us."

Audra let out a surprised laugh. "*You* want to speak to a therapist?"

His lips flattened.

"You have to admit, that's shocking."

"I'll do anything for my kids."

Slapping her would have been kinder.

With renewed anger, she tilted her chin higher. "What if I don't want to go to counseling?"

Damon shoved a hand deep into one pocket. He seemed taller and more intimidating and frowned at her in a way that made her want to run and hide. But she wouldn't. She steeled her spine and stared directly in his eyes.

"I'm not going to let you have my kids just like that."

Her belly tanked at the iron in his tone and the obvious threat of a pending battle. "Are you threatening me?" She never knew this side of him existed.

"I'm letting you know that I'm not giving up without a fight. *We* shouldn't give up without a fight. Till death do us part, Audra. That's what we agreed to. We should do everything we can to keep our family together and protect our kids before we divorce. I know I can't make you do this, but I'm letting you know right now, we either fight for our marriage, or we fight for our kids. The choice is yours."

They stared at each other. He with an icy calm, she with a quivering fear, knowing she risked losing not only her husband, but her children.

"I need to sleep on it." She couldn't think straight in her current state of emotional turmoil.

"Do that. Give me your answer tomorrow."

Damon slid the door open.

"Six weeks?" Audra asked.

"Yes."

"What if she c-can't help us?"

A strange emotion she didn't recognize crossed his face.

Damon swallowed. "Then we walk away and bring in the lawyers."

Chapter Fifteen

A day trip to Miami was exactly the escape Audra needed.

La Comida Deliciosa, located on the popular South Beach strip, served yummy tapas and potent drinks—at least, according to her younger sister, Monica.

Monica had invited Audra and Skye to Miami because last time she visited, she enjoyed eating at the casual dining restaurant and craved the food again. Since her boyfriend, Andre, couldn't make the trip because of work obligations, she invited Audra and Skye to accompany her. After lunch, they planned to do a little shopping and then return to Atlanta.

They sat at a table on the upper level with a view of the strip and the water. All around them, diners noshed their lunches, drank colorful drinks, and engaged in lively conversation.

Monica, fabulous, as usual, wore a hot pink halter top jumpsuit and huge, multicolored earrings that brightened her face. Very South Beach.

Audra had opted for comfort and wore brown linen pants

with a drawstring, a loose-fitting white top, and sandals. She held her hair back from her face with large sunglasses perched on her head. She took a sip of water and perused the menu. "What are you two having?"

"I called ahead and ordered two servings of the Spanish meatballs for the table. They are *so* delicious. I'm having the pan-seared chicken with steamed rice for my meal," Monica said.

"Good idea to call ahead. I'm starving!" Skye exclaimed with a smile as bright as the yellow diamond on her finger. She had styled her hair in big curls and also fit the South Beach aesthetic in a floral print skirt and lavender top that worked well against her golden skin.

Audra skimmed the description of her sister's meal. "That chicken sounds good. The dish includes ham. Hmm..."

"I'm going to make a meal out of several tapas." Satisfied with her decision, Skye placed her menu on the table.

Skye had been in their lives so long, she was part of the family, so whenever the three dined together, they made an effort to order different meals so they could try each other's food.

"Steak with cheese grits and vegetables," Audra announced, setting aside her menu.

"I almost ordered that," Monica said.

The server arrived and took their orders, returning a few minutes later with a pitcher of sangria. Before they filled their glasses, Monica snapped a photo for her Instagram page.

Audra sipped the drink, letting out a surprised whimper at the delicious flavor.

"Guess what? I started the hunt for a new assistant. One of Ignacio's actor friends recommended someone to me, and I talked to her. She's very efficient," Monica said.

"Why did his friend let her go?" Audra asked.

"He hired a family member who needed the work."

"At least he didn't let her go for some other reason," Skye said with meaning.

Monica's relationship with her last assistant, Daisy, fell apart in a spectacular way.

"I know." Remembering the fall out, Monica shivered. "This woman looks good on paper, but I'm not sure if I should include her in the list of finalists. She's a little older—mid-forties. I doubt we can be friends. I don't think she'll *get* me." She wrinkled her nose.

"The last thing you need is a friend as your employee. Look at what happened last time," Audra reminded her.

"True." Monica pursed her lips.

"Why don't you do a test run? Have a probationary period. That way you both know it might not lead to more, but if you work well together, you can keep her permanently."

Monica nodded. "That's normally what I do, but I'm worried about the age difference."

"She might work better for you. More mature, and if her references are solid, why would her age matter? You need her to run errands and assist you. Anyone can do that once you train them to your work style."

Monica nodded. "You're right. I'm worried about nothing. How's the wedding planning going?" she asked Skye.

Pretending to choke on the sangria, Audra coughed and smacked her chest. She carefully placed her glass on the table. "Excuse me? Did you ask the bride-to-be about her wedding plans?"

In the past, Monica had acted as if she was allergic to marriage.

"Will wonders never cease," Skye said.

"Very funny, you two. Give me the update without all the extra, please." Monica rolled her eyes.

Laughing, Skye reached across the table and patted Monica's hand. "We couldn't help but tease you. We've settled on a venue, and now I'm working on the menu, but I haven't found a dress. I can't believe how difficult this part is. I assumed I'd find the perfect dress right away."

"What about the one you sent me a picture of when you and Mom went to New York? I liked that one," Audra said.

"I'm leaning toward it, but I'm not sure. The dress didn't feel perfect, you know?" Skye pulled out her phone and took a look at the photo of her in the dress. The off-the-shoulder gown flattered her voluptuous figure.

Audra experienced a twinge of envy. From a young age, she anticipated getting married and, as a teen, planned all the details of her wedding. Rose gold dresses and a gorgeous bouquet with pinks, yellows, and light orange. A summer ceremony, no fewer than six bridesmaids. But she never had the opportunity to go through the ritual of dress shopping or menu planning. When Damon found out she was pregnant with Junior, he proposed right away, and they married at the courthouse. A shotgun wedding, but they held the gun.

She shoved aside her envy and concentrated on comforting Skye. "When you find the right dress, you'll know. The clouds will part, and sunshine will pour out of the sky onto your head."

They all giggled.

"I hope you're right." Skye put away her phone.

By the time the food came, they were on the topic of their mother, Rose, who would be taking off around the Fourth of July for a two-week vacation with friends in the Greek islands.

"I'm glad she's going on the trip," Skye said, spooning octopus salad onto Monica's plate and then Audra's.

"I've been thinking about introducing her to my neighbor. He's a widow. What do you guys think?" Audra asked.

"Slow your roll," Monica said. "Did you know Papa Ben is going on the trip?"

Audra blinked. "I didn't know that."

"Since when does Benicio take vacations?" Skye asked.

Covering her mouth, Monica finished chewing before she responded. "Since he found out his friends invited a man on the trip to keep Mommy company." She arched an eyebrow.

"They invited another man on the trip?" Skye asked.

Monica nodded vigorously.

Audra snorted and then covered her face. "No."

"You're kidding," Skye added.

"I'm not," Monica sang.

The three of them had a good laugh.

Monica waved over the server and requested another pitcher of sangria.

Audra propped her chin on her hand. "I would love to be a fly on the cabin wall to see what happens."

"Benicio is a hoot. Why would he think being the fifth wheel is okay?" Skye asked.

"Because he's stubborn as hell and won't admit he wants to be with Mommy. She's the same way. Maybe this trip will force them to face reality, so hold off on your neighbor, Audra." Monica sipped her drink.

"I will, but I don't know about Mom and Benicio getting back together," Audra hedged. "Like you said, they're both pretty stubborn and have dated other people since the divorce, but I'd still love to know what happens on the trip."

"I got you. When Mommy comes back, I'll drill her for the deets and let you know."

"When you call Audra, call me too. I want to know every-thing," Skye interjected.

"Deal. Oh, before I forget, I need to ask your opinion." Monica leaned forward in earnest, eyes getting brighter. "I have this brilliant idea for the opening of Andre's lounge. Every day during opening week, a different celebrity pops in to party and have drinks. I already spoke to Ignacio, and he's going to show up and bring a few A-listers. Do you think Damon would be interested in coming and bringing some of his friends?" She turned expectant eyes on Audra.

NV Lounge, her boyfriend's project, would essentially be a competitor against his former boss's similar location catering to young Black professionals with disposable income. Located in an up-and-coming part of the city, they fully expected it to be a success because of Andre's work experience, and Monica planned to help him with publicity as much as she could.

"I can't speak for Damon, but I don't think he would mind attending, as long as there's no conflict on his calendar. He could probably round up a few of the players to come with him."

Monica let out a quiet squeal and shimmied in her chair. "That would be perfect. When would be a good time to call him?"

"Whenever." Audra shrugged. She didn't want to talk about her husband anymore. The topic was bringing her down.

"Okay, I'll check in with Andre and see what he can offer in the way of VIP treatment, and then I'll give Damon a call."

Skye popped a piece of bread topped with chorizo, ham, and melted cheese into her mouth. "What plans do you have with the kids this summer?" she asked Audra, her words garbled as she chewed.

"They're in camp, and Damon's parents want them to come to Arkansas for a week or two."

"I'd be happy to take them off your hands whenever you and Damon need a break," Skye offered.

She had babysat for them in the past, much to Kerilyn's

chagrin, who believed she was old enough to keep watch of her younger siblings for a few hours.

"It's been awhile since you've watched them, hasn't it?" Audra asked.

"A long time. Unless you and Damon have gotten someone else to watch them, you must be desperate for alone time," Skye said with a laugh.

Audra dipped her gaze away from Skye's smiling face to her plate.

"Did I say something wrong?" Skye asked.

Audra blinked rapidly. "No. I'm fine."

She lifted her glass and chugged the sangria.

The silence let her know her behavior shocked the other two women at the table, but she couldn't look at them. She was in her feelings, filled with weepy emotions she'd pushed down but now bubbled to the surface at a seriously inopportune time.

She poured another glass of sangria from the fresh pitcher the waitress had dropped off. Maybe she could numb the pain with alcohol. She brought the glass to her lips, but Monica eased the drink away from her mouth.

"Okay, that's enough," her younger sister said.

"I was drinking that," Audra said.

Monica set the glass to her right, out of Audra's reach. "What's going on?"

Audra looked at her sister. Then she looked at Skye.

The combination of their concerned expressions and her emotional state shattered her fragile mask of serenity like a hammer against thin glass.

She burst into tears.

Chapter Sixteen

Audra splashed water on her face in the bathroom and then dabbed away the droplets. Listening to Monica and Skye's murmurs of concern had only made her cry more.

After an embarrassing display of weeping at the table, with Skye rubbing her back and Monica demanding to know what the hell was going on, Audra finally excused herself. When they both rose to follow her, she insisted they remain in their chairs and promised to be right back.

Taking a deep breath, she replaced the sunglasses on her head and then prepared to face them. In the dining room, she gave a weak smile to the waitress, who watched her with wary concern. Goodness, she'd made such a spectacle of herself, sobbing over her meal in the middle of the restaurant. The burn of the other diners' eyes hit the back of her head as she made her way to the table.

She sat down and fixed a smile on her face. "I'm fine."

"No, you're not," the other two said at the same time.

"You might as well tell us what's going on," Monica added.

Audra fiddled with the white napkin across her thighs. She didn't want to divulge her problems to them. She was embarrassed. Years ago, she had been well aware of the whispers and gossip blog articles that insinuated Damon had only married her because she became pregnant. Now, here they were, almost nine years later, getting the divorce that seemed portentous from the moment they said, "I do."

"Damon and I are having problems," she reluctantly admitted.

A brief pause as the other two absorbed the information.

"How bad is it?" Monica asked.

"I asked for a divorce."

Both women gasped.

"No," Skye whispered.

Audra nodded, unable to speak as emotion burned her throat again.

Monica replaced the glass of sangria in front of her. "You definitely need this."

Audra smiled weakly.

"That's why he fell off from attending family events?" her sister asked.

Audra nodded. "I stopped going to his events too. Being together has become so uncomfortable, like we don't know what to do when we're alone together. When we do talk to each other, we end up in tense arguments that lead nowhere."

"What caused this?" Skye asked.

Audra swallowed the lump in her throat. "You know we've been trying to have more children, and... I've had three miscarriages."

Skye gasped and placed a hand on her shoulder. "Oh, sweetheart, I knew about the one, but I didn't know you'd had two more."

"No one did."

"I'm so sorry."

"It's been hard, and that's when I believe the problems started. We drifted away from each other, and the last six months have been the absolute worst. The weight of our losses over the past couple years... the burden of our pain... became unbearable."

"I had no idea," Monica said quietly.

Audra hated to bring them down during a day earmarked for fun, but she'd suffered in silence for a long time.

"I don't understand why I can't carry a pregnancy to term. I've had three babies, no problem, and then that kept happening. I want an explanation."

"What do the doctors say?" Monica asked.

"They've run all kinds of tests but couldn't find anything definitive they could point to and say *this* is the problem. Meanwhile, Damon and I have drifted further apart. Our relationship is in shambles. We haven't had sex in months."

Skye's eyes widened. "You're kidding."

"I wish."

Sex had become less an act of pleasure and more about achieving pregnancy. A chore, a means to an end, instead of a beautiful expression of their love.

"Have you tried counseling?" Monica asked.

"Yes, actually. Damon suggested we try," Audra admitted. "We met with a counselor, a woman by the name of Dr. Lewis. One of our friends recommended her. In the first meeting, we got to know her, set the time and day for our regular sessions, and determined if we were a good fit."

The forty-five-minute session passed quickly, with the therapist giving them a homework assignment to go on a dinner date. Audra had dreaded going out with Damon alone, and rightfully so. They had barely talked. She didn't look forward to giving the therapist an update at the next appointment

"Are you going back?" Monica asked.

"Yes," Audra replied.

"Since you're going back, that's a good sign, right?" Skye asked.

Audra let out a short, humorless laugh. "Not really. We've only had the one session, but I think it's a waste of time. Damon clearly doesn't want to be there, but we committed to trying for at least six weeks."

"Why six weeks?"

"That's the amount of time Dr. Lewis claims she needs to be able to help us."

"She must be really good," Skye remarked.

"Whether or not she is, I'm over it," Audra said.

"What do you mean you're over it?" her sister asked.

"I agreed to participate in six weeks of therapy, and I'll do my part, but Damon and I are miles away from where we used to be as a couple. Most of the time, he ignores me. He stays out late, and since the divorce talk, he permanently moved into one of the spare bedrooms."

"Oh my goodness," Skye muttered.

"What did he say when you asked for a divorce?" Monica asked.

Audra drank a mouthful of flavorful sangria before she divulged the painful truth. "One of the first things out of his mouth was that I was not going to keep him from his kids. The children are his priority, and I understand that. They're my priority too. But what about me? It's like he doesn't give a damn about me. He said *I* should move out, and he'll stay in the house with the kids."

"*What?*" Monica said.

Audra's gaze jumped from Monica's horror-stricken face to Skye's horror-stricken face. "I don't matter to him anymore. All he cares about is Junior, Tracy, and Keri, and I... I'm jealous.

What kind of mother is jealous of her own children?" Fresh tears sprang to Audra's eyes, and she dabbed them away with the napkin.

"Asshole." Monica's lips firmed into a tight line.

Audra recognized the determined glint in her sister's eyes. An angry Monica meant a meddling Monica. "Do not," she warned.

Ever defiant, her sister averted her gaze to the beach across the street with an obstinate tilt of her chin.

"*Monica.*" Audra grabbed her wrist.

"Fine, I won't interfere, and I won't cuss him out, though he deserves it." She pursed her lips.

"Thank you. Damon and I are going to handle this problem ourselves."

"It's perfectly natural to feel jealous," Skye said, "especially when your husband has been ignoring you, and clearly, he's been ignoring you for a while."

Audra pressed her fingertips to her temples in a vain attempt to alleviate a pending headache. "I need to get through the next five weeks, and then I'll know what to do."

"Have you spoken to an attorney yet?"

Audra nodded. "Yes, but I'm holding off for now."

After Audra told Damon she would attend the therapy sessions, she contacted Faydra and let her know she needed to postpone the divorce. The attorney said she understood and encouraged her to save her marriage if she could. If she couldn't, she would be ready and available to help.

"Is there anything I can do?" Skye asked.

"I appreciate the two of you listening to me, but this problem belongs to me and Damon."

"People turn into monsters when they divorce. Seems he already has," Monica muttered.

"He'll do what's right for our children, and so will I."

Opening up about her problems and her plans improved Audra's mood a little. Some of the burden had lifted from her shoulders.

"Do you think the two of you will be able to reconcile?" Skye asked, sadness in her voice.

"Unless we have a major breakthrough in therapy, I don't see reconciliation in our future. So often people stay together for the wrong reasons. You have to know when to quit and walk away."

Chapter Seventeen

Week number two.

Audra sat stiffly on the cream sofa in the therapist's office, fingers threaded together on her lap.

In the first meeting, the doctor had introduced herself and her methodology. She'd been empathetic with a soothing voice. She had, however, asked a question at the end which continued to gnaw at Audra.

"If you could marry each other again today, would you? Don't answer but think about it. Not every couple should stay together. If your answer is no right now, my job is to find out if that answer could become a yes."

Audra's answer was no and doubted it could become a yes. What was Damon's answer? No as well, no doubt.

The first session had done nothing to bridge the chasm between them. In fact, the hole appeared wider and harder to cross. He sat in silence beside her, staring straight ahead. They had barely spoken since their arrival for the appointment and rode in separate cars on the way there. She didn't mind because riding together would have been scream-inducing.

Audra glanced at the door and rubbed her hands together.

Where is Dr. Lewis? she thought.

"Did you work out today?" she asked, to fill the lack of sound in the room.

Damon shifted on the seat. "Yeah."

The bass in his voice sent a tremor through her. One single word had such a profound effect.

"How was it?"

To encourage communication, the therapist had advised them to ask follow-up questions.

"Good. Did you work on the blog today?" He glanced at her.

She hated the way he looked *through* her instead of at her.

"Yes."

"How was it?"

"Good," she answered, swallowing past the thickness in her throat. That seemed to be their favorite word nowadays. A meaningless, hollow, empty word. "I got a lot done this morning after you and the kids left."

He slowly nodded his head, but she doubted he cared one way or the other about her morning. They no longer hung on each other's every word.

Out of ideas to initiate conversation, Audra glanced at the door, twisting her wedding rings on her finger as she impatiently waited for their counselor to enter. If forced to endure much more of this uncomfortable situation, she would end up losing her mind.

The door burst open, and Dr. Lewis rushed in. "Sorry to keep you waiting," she said in a breathless voice.

A Black woman with wheat-colored skin, she wore a violet pantsuit cinched to one side of her slim waist. Her raven hair was in a messy bun, and her black glasses rested on a nose spattered with freckles.

"It's okay," Damon and Audra murmured at the same time.

"I had a bit of an emergency with one of my other clients. A minor meltdown that hopefully has been resolved. Can I get you anything to drink?"

"I'm fine." Audra lifted an eight-ounce bottle of water from the table beside the sofa, which she had taken from the small refrigerator in the corner.

"Damon, are you okay?"

"I'm good."

Dr. Lewis gave them a brief smile before unlocking her desk and removing a padded notebook and pen. She settled in the chair across the cocktail table from them and tucked an errant strand of hair behind her ear. She then crossed one leg over the other.

"Let's get started. At the end of last week's meeting, I gave you homework to do. You were supposed to go on a date. Did you do that?"

They both nodded.

"When did you go out?"

"Thursday night," Audra answered.

"What did you do?"

"We went to dinner," Audra replied.

"How was dinner?"

"Good," Audra and Damon said at the same time.

The doctor's lips transformed into the faintest smile. "What was good about the date, Damon?"

He rubbed the back of his neck. "The food. The wine. The restaurant was nice."

"Anything else?"

He shrugged.

He couldn't be more obvious that he didn't want to be

there. Why did he suggest counseling if he didn't intend to put in the effort?

"Okay, Audra, what did you enjoy about the date?"

"The same things. The food and wine were excellent. The waiter suggested a nice chardonnay, which I enjoyed. I had three glasses." She let out a little laugh. "We lucked out and were seated at a great table which gave us a view of the entire restaurant and the street outside. Considering the place was newly opened, I was impressed by the level of service and the delicious food. I had the gnocchi."

"I'm happy to hear you both enjoyed the food and the ambiance. According to our previous conversation, every time you go out to dinner, your children are with you. As you know, the point of that exercise was to have you do an activity together, the two of you, without the children, giving you a chance to spend time alone, as a couple. What did you talk about?"

Damon glanced at Audra, so she answered. "Work. The kids, mostly," she admitted with an embarrassed laugh. "We, um... I don't think we did a very good job with the homework assignment."

They didn't enjoy dinner without the kids. The so-called date had been terribly awkward. She and Damon barely talked, with long lapses of silence filled by the buzz of conversation and clatter of silverware against plates around them. She used to love dressing up in lovely dresses and jewelry, going out and spending time with him.

Yet last week, she had been desperate for the night to end. When the waiter arrived at the end of the meal, they both hastily agreed they didn't want dessert, relieved when he brought the check, and they could finally escape each other's company.

"Was conversation difficult?" Dr. Lewis asked gently.

Audra's throat tightened with emotion. "Yes."

"How was it for you?" The doctor directed her attention to Damon.

His jaw tightened. "Like she said, difficult. Awkward."

Sadness filled her. She bit her bottom lip to stop its trembling.

"The good news is, you both agree that conversation was difficult. That's a good thing, though it might not seem that way. Your responses mean you're on the same page, and acknowledging your sameness is an important part of bridging the divide in your marriage. If one of you had said the night went well and the other said it was awkward, I'd be concerned. But your answers tell me that you're in agreement that something is *wrong*. That's very important."

Though not news to them, Audra let the words sink in.

"Let's move on from dating for now. I asked you to bring two copies of a photo from your wedding day. Did you bring them?"

"Yes." Audra pulled the photos from her purse and handed them to Dr. Lewis.

"Great. How did you feel that day? Audra, you first." Dr. Lewis held up one photo to face them.

They stood side by side with the officiant. It was hard to tell in the photo because she hadn't gained as much weight with Junior as she did with Tracy, but she was already five months pregnant.

"Nervous."

"Give me a positive word."

Audra resisted the urge to roll her eyes in frustration. "Hopeful."

"Why hopeful?"

"We kinda rushed into marriage because I was pregnant, and I wanted everything to be okay. With the pregnancy.

With our marriage. I wasn't sure if we'd made the right decision."

"You thought maybe the marriage wouldn't last?"

Audra nodded.

"Then why'd you say yes?" Damon asked, sounding offended.

"Why do you think?" Audra shot back.

"Remember, no assumptions. Tell him why, Audra," Dr. Lewis prodded gently.

She dropped her gaze to her hands. The good doctor had chided them that assumptions were based on personal perceptions and almost always wrong. She suggested honesty and speaking directly to avoid misunderstandings.

"I was in love with him."

"Tell *him*."

With difficulty, she looked at Damon, and her insides tightened. "I was in love with you."

A muscle in his jaw tightened and his Adam's apple bobbed up and down.

"What made you fall in love with him?"

"He did sweet things."

"Such as?"

Audra smiled faintly at the memories. "He knew I liked jelly beans and would show up with these little packets of jelly beans and hand them to me. It was nice. Thoughtful."

Damon shifted in the chair.

Dr. Lewis nodded. "What else caused you to fall in love with him?"

"We used to talk all the time. Well, I talked mostly, but we'd be on the phone for hours. During his away games, he kept me on the phone long after he should. Sometimes I worried our late nights would affect his game. Even after we got married, he seemed to want to talk to me. I'd be changing the baby's diaper in the nursery, and he'd stand in the doorway chatting me up."

"Did you enjoy those conversations?" Dr. Lewis asked.

"Yes."

She always wanted to be near him. If he were tinkering with tools in the yard, she'd mosey on out there with something to drink or a snack, and they'd end up sitting on rusty stools and talking for an eternity. Nowadays though, they were seldom in the same room as each other. In fact, he seemed to make a point not to be in the same room as her, and every time he left her space, her heart cracked in a different place.

"Do you miss that?" Dr. Lewis asked gently.

With emotion clogging her throat, Audra couldn't respond. She didn't want to answer any more questions. She pulled her lips in and simply nodded.

Dr. Lewis must have sensed her need for respite because she turned her attention to Damon.

"Why did you spend so much time talking to Audra?"

He shrugged. "I liked the sound of her voice."

"Is that the only reason?"

He paused.

"I liked hearing stories about her family. What they were getting into, plans for the future, that kind of thing. Also, because no matter how terrible my day at practice or during a game, talking to her made me feel better. She was positive all the damn time. Sweet-natured."

"How did you feel on this day when you married her? Use a positive word."

He stared at the photo. "Excited."

"Tell me more."

He rubbed the back of his neck again. "I ah... I guess I was looking forward to having a family. Different from the one I had before... before I was adopted."

"You were adopted?" Dr. Lewis's eyebrows lifted higher.

"Yes," he answered in a clipped tone.

He was about to shut down because he didn't like talking about his past. Audra's hand itched to reach for his and provide comfort. Instead, she fisted her fingers in her lap.

Wisely, the doctor moved on. "Did you ask Audra to marry you because she was pregnant?"

"I asked her to marry me *at that time* because she was pregnant, but that's not why I wanted to marry her."

"Tell her why you wanted to marry her."

He glanced at her. "I was in love with you."

Dr. Lewis scribbled some notes.

Hearing Damon say he married her for love—not simply because she was pregnant—eased some of the doubts in Audra's mind. They had both loved each other when they married, but that didn't mean things couldn't change.

The session continued for another thirty minutes. At the end, Dr. Lewis closed her notebook.

"This week's homework assignment is easy. I want you each to take this photo and sit with it in your car for five minutes. Think about your excitement and hope for your future marriage. Connect with those feelings again. On the drive home, Damon give Audra a call. Talk to her, like you did before you were married. Tell her what's going on at work, and Audra catch him up on the latest with your family. I'll see you both at the same time next week."

Chapter Eighteen

Damon slumped in the driver's seat of the Range Rover.

I was in love with you.

Was.

Past tense. He'd said the same thing, but like a broken record, his brain remained stuck on Audra saying the word.

He stared at the image of him and Audra together. They both looked so young, eyes bright with expectations for the future. Bright with love.

Audra hadn't mentioned this during their session, but they had fallen asleep several times on the phone, like teenagers who couldn't stand to hang up.

Before her, he went through women quickly and with all the arrogance afforded a wealthy athlete, but when Audra became pregnant, he jumped at the chance to marry her and start a family of his own. He looked forward to becoming a member of her large family, whose branches stretched throughout the South and extended all the way to Mexico through her stepfather.

She had become his best friend. How had everything gotten so fucked up?

He slammed his fist on the steering wheel and stared out the window.

He had an assignment. Dr. Lewis said he needed to call his wife and talk, so he'd do that.

Damon started the car and dialed Audra's number as he pulled out of the parking space.

"Hello?"

Her voice did things to him. He imagined her warm breath on his neck as she whispered one of her corny jokes in his ear, laughing the whole time because she thought she was some kind of comedian. She told the worst jokes, sometimes messing up the punchline, but he couldn't help but laugh because she was so darn cute.

"Hey. Where are you?"

"On the road already," Audra answered.

"You going back to the house?"

"No, I'm going to stop by the store first. Our grocery delivery was missing a few items that I need for dinner."

Damon rolled his neck. *Come on, you can do this.*

"Did they ever find someone to replace the other guy? What was his name?"

"Levon. They did."

"You got him trained yet?"

Audra was very particular about her grocery items, especially the produce.

He heard a brief sound of laughter, which prompted a smile to his own face. He could imagine her eyes lighting up, her luscious lips stretched briefly across her face in amusement.

"Not yet, but I'm working on him."

"For his sake, I hope he learns fast."

"Am I that bad?"

"I don't think it's bad, but you don't play about your fruits and vegetables."

There was a momentary pause, and Damon slowed for a pedestrian in the crosswalk.

"Are you headed home?" Audra asked.

"I'm going by the office to check for mail and pick up a file I want to review later tonight. While I'm there, I'll get a sandwich at the shop down the street."

Then he remembered the comment about the jelly beans. She enjoyed the candy so much because her biological father used to sneak them to her against her mother's wishes. Those bite-size pieces of sugar embedded a positive memory in her brain of the man who was no longer alive. So, Damon bought a big ole box of mini-packs and randomly gave them to her. She always used to grin or do a little dance, as if he'd handed her a bag of diamonds.

"You want me to get you a sandwich?" he asked.

Silence.

"Um, yes. If you don't mind." She sounded surprised.

How pathetic that he had surprised his wife by offering to buy her a damn sandwich?

"Of course, I don't mind, Audra." *Don't start an argument. Don't start an argument.* "You want the Reuben sandwich?"

"Yes. On—"

"On rye with two pickles. I know."

He had ordered sandwiches for her from the same shop for years. There was no way he could forget her order.

"That's right."

Her voice sounded soft and achingly sweet, and he suddenly wished he could see her face. His fingers tightened around the steering wheel. He couldn't get enough of watching her do anything—eat, drink, walk, talk, cry out beneath him. Man, he missed her. Missed *them* and what they used to share.

"What did you think about today's session?" Audra asked in a tentative voice.

Talk. It's not that hard, Damon told himself.

"The session went well. She got me thinking about some things."

"Me too." Pause. "Did I really make you feel better when you were down?"

He smiled briefly. "Every single time. You might not remember this, but when we lost the game against the Red Sox, I was pissed because I saw my chance for a division title slipping away."

"I remember."

"Do you remember what you told me when I called?"

"Not really."

"You reminded me of what a great player I was and rattled off a bunch of my stats. It wasn't just that you were trying to cheer me up. You actually knew my stats, but when we met, you didn't know anything about baseball. You didn't even know who I was. You made an effort, which was important to me."

"What kind of wife would I be if I showed zero interest in what you were doing?"

"I don't think you understand how much that influenced my mood. And your confidence in me, made me feel confident. Anyway, that made my job easier, to go out there and kick ass in the next game."

"Are you saying you won the East Division title because of my pep talk?"

Eyes on the road ahead, he laughed. "Don't go getting a big head, but your pep talk might have helped a little bit. In addition to all the training, advice from the coach, and watching videos of the game—and of course, my teammates."

"All very minor, I'm sure."

This was the Audra he'd missed. The funny, light-hearted

woman. She'd disappeared behind a moody, miserable woman who didn't want to be touched and was defensive all the time.

"I'm at the office. I'll run upstairs and then get our sandwiches and come home."

"Okay, see you later." She was smiling. He could tell by her voice.

He used to get deep belly laughs from her, but now she rarely smiled. At least at him. Everyone else, including their neighbors and the grocery delivery man got her smiles. This was momentous.

Damon took the elevator to his office but didn't stay long. He strolled in, chatted with his small staff of two for a few minutes, and then went into his personal office. He flipped through the mail, pausing for a moment to look at an invitation to an event he and Audra had attended in the past.

As the day drew nearer and their relationship remained cool, he had considered going by himself. Maybe he and Audra should go together and have a second shot at a date night of sorts.

He gathered up the mail and left the office.

"Damon, did you check your email?" Bea, his office manager and assistant, called as he passed by.

He backed up and peered into her office. "No."

"They sent over the final images for the Calvin Klein campaign." She walked over with the iPad she carried everywhere. Showing him the screen, she slowly scrolled through the images.

"I like them all. What do you think?" Damon asked.

"They're all well done. These two will be part of the print campaign, and this one will go on the billboards." She pointed at a photo of him looking into the camera, his jeans unzipped and exposing blue boxer briefs with the Calvin Klein waistband.

"They look great," Damon said.

"Good. I'll tell them we're good to go."

"That's all you need from me?"

"Yes. Are you coming back later?"

Damon paused. "No. Call if you need me."

"Will do."

Damon left and made a beeline for the sandwich shop a couple blocks away. Once he had the order, he returned to the Range Rover and took off for home.

He entered the kitchen from the garage and found Audra stirring a large pitcher of iced tea.

Instead of the usual indifference, her eyes softened and her lips curled into a smile. His gaze lingered on the contour and shape of her mouth. The provocative tilt of her lush lips called to him. Enticed him.

"I made tea."

He held up the bag with the food. "Sandwiches."

"We can eat outside on the patio. It's not very hot right now." Audra dropped ice cubes into two glasses.

"Sounds good. Let me have some of that."

She poured some tea and slid the glass over.

His eyes latched on to her engagement ring and wedding ring. He had agonized over them. Despite the short notice, choosing the right jewelry had not been a quick decision. The wedding ring was a plain platinum band. The engagement ring consisted of a round cut diamond set in a platinum band. It was brilliant, but to this day, he wasn't sure he'd chosen well despite Audra saying she loved the set.

"Thanks." With a few gulps, he drained the glass. "Dang, that's some good tea."

She poured him another glass and one for herself, then they went outside and sat on the padded bench on the patio. They set their plates and drinks on the low table in front of them.

140

Seated at the other end of the bench, she seemed so far away, but he knew better than to make a fuss. They were trying, and this was the first time in a long time they had been together alone without frigid air between them.

They ate in silence for a moment.

"When was the last time you had one of those sandwiches?" Damon asked.

"I can't remember, but it's so good." She hummed her satisfaction.

His eyes snagged on a dot of sauce at the corner of her mouth. "You have a little sauce right there."

Audra dabbed at her mouth with a napkin and got rid of the sauce. "Did I get it?"

He didn't miss a beat with the lie. "Nah. I'll get it for you."

His thumb swept the corner of her lips. She let him touch her—without recoiling or tensing. His body experienced a heated reawakening, as if jolted out of hibernation.

"There. Got it," he said huskily.

Audra dipped her gaze, which meant he couldn't read her expression. "Thanks." Her voice sounded a little breathless.

Down boy, Damon silently warned his excited penis.

He bit into his steak sandwich and chewed for a minute, savoring the silence. Not awkward like the other night at dinner. Much more comfortable.

"Oh, I almost forgot. I have the invitation for the Children's Cancer Society fundraiser."

Each year they and their friends Simon and Elsa alternated paying for a table and invited the other couple to join them.

"You want to go this year?" Audra asked.

"Yeah, don't you?"

"I do."

"So, we're going, right?"

"We haven't missed in all these years, and I don't think we

should start now. Maybe we can mention the event to Dr. Lewis at next week's session." She raised her eyebrows in question.

"Good idea."

As he continued eating, he became aware that they were having a normal conversation which hadn't devolved into anger or an argument.

They were only two counseling sessions in.

Chapter Nineteen

D ay two of her vacation, Rose stepped out of the cabin of Sylvie Johnson's yacht, only a mile from the nearest Greek island in the calm, cerulean waters of the Aegean Sea. A nice breeze fluttered her hair and her loose-fitting, powder-blue ensemble—pants and a short-sleeved over-sized blouse that landed mid-thigh.

The sleek yacht included six staterooms able to accommodate up to twelve occupants. At the moment, Benicio, Oscar Brooks—Sylvie's husband—and the male guest, George, whom they had invited to keep Rose company, were seated on the large sun deck as they watched the waning daylight. The men smoked cigars and sipped Glenlivet whiskey, talking and laughing like old friends.

Sylvie joined her outside. "Here you go, darling," she said in her cultured voice, handing Rose a glass of white wine.

The billionaire entrepreneur was stunning with her thick raven hair pulled back from her face in one long braid. Her dark-brown skin contrasted with shrewd, light-brown eyes.

Stylishly casual, she wore white capris and a white shirt, setting them off with a gold belt and matching jewelry.

"This is so bizarre." Rose sipped the wine, eyeing her ex-husband and the two men.

"I thought the same thing when Oscar told me that Benicio asked for an invitation. Of course, I was appalled. That's why I warned you immediately because I didn't want you to be blindsided."

"Ben insisted Oscar invited him."

"Interesting. Oscar insists Benicio *demanded* to be invited. Whatever happened, I'm glad you didn't cancel."

Rose inhaled the salty sea air. "I couldn't miss this. It's so lovely here, and I'm excited for the rest of my vacation. If I haven't said so already, thank you for the invitation."

"Of course. I thought it would be nice to have you along and perhaps meeting a nice man at the same time wouldn't hurt."

Rose allowed a soft smile to touch the corners of her lips. "George is nice. I hope he's not uncomfortable with Ben here, though he seems fine. You know..." She dropped her voice, and Sylvie drew closer. "The interesting part of this whole debacle is that Ben took time off—more time than I've seen him take in years. What prompted him to do so now?"

Sylvie arched an eyebrow. "You don't know?" she asked in an amused tone.

"I think I do, but it doesn't make sense."

"He's here because of *you*, darling. Because he doesn't want to risk losing you for good. While you're at the house puttering around your garden, enjoying meals with the family, and planning your eldest son's wedding, he can keep tabs on you. He can*not* keep tabs on you when you're in the middle of the Aegean Sea with another man and possibly falling for him. He may be your ex-husband according to the courts, but I do believe *he* considers you still married."

Rose blushed and shook her head. "That's preposterous, considering he's admitted to me that he's dated, and so have I."

"That doesn't change how he feels in his heart. Look at Oscar and I. We were divorced for fifteen years, had both been involved with other people, yet here we are—back together again." Sylvie glanced in the direction of her husband, and her features softened.

"I want to believe you, but I know Benicio. He... I don't know. We're so different, sometimes I wonder if..."

Sylvie paused with her glass of wine halfway to her mouth. "What?"

"He has a big personality and much like you, he's wealthy and fabulous." She laughed, recalling one of their first dates. "When we first met, he took me to this expensive restaurant. I felt so out of place in my Marshalls dress. So gauche, and he was kind despite all my flubs. I enjoyed his company but assumed he wouldn't call again."

Sylvie watched her intently. "But...?"

Rose's smile widened, and her heart warmed at the memory. "He called the very next day."

She and her dead husband had more in common, coming from the same background. Yet for some reason, she and Benicio had connected from that first date.

"You sound surprised," Sylvie said in her cultured voice.

"I guess I was. Still am in some ways," Rose murmured.

"You think he's too good for you."

"No, nothing like that," Rose denied hastily.

"Then you think you don't fit in. Is that it?"

Sylvie was too perceptive.

Loathed to admit her feelings, Rose remained silent.

"I don't have a lot of friends," Sylvie said slowly, thought-fully. "I've seen the avarice in humans. We are imperfect crea-tures—greedy, unkind, selfish. There are very few people who I really trust. My husband is one of the few, and for many years, I didn't have him before we found our way back together. I gave him a hell of a time because of my doubts. Finding people to trust can be difficult and, in some ways, worse in our world. I'm sure you see it. There's always someone with their hand out or a trick up their sleeve. But every once in a while, you come across a good person. Someone genuine, who is kind and generous and wants the best for you, and then you hold on to that person as tight as you can without suffocating them—which isn't always easy." She laughed.

"You're a good person, Rose. That's why I like you. That's why I enjoy spending time with you. That's why Benicio is in love with you. He never cared about where you came from or what you wore. I'm sure he didn't care when he saw you in your Marshalls dress. Because he saw *you*—a woman who would love his children as her own and whose children he could love. A woman he could build a life with. I don't know what's going on inside his head at the moment, but I assure you, you fit perfectly inside his world."

Emotional, Rose squeezed her friend's hand. "Thank you. I needed that."

"You're welcome, my darling."

"For the record, you've been a very good friend to me. I appreciate your kindness."

"Oscar says I'm kind to people I like and indifferent to everyone else. I told him that's who I am."

"So, I'm lucky, then. Special, even."

"Very, according to Oscar," Sylvie said with a twinkle in her eye. She looped arms with Rose. "Let's see what these men are up to, shall we?"

They strolled across the deck and joined the conversation with the men.

Chapter Twenty

"How did last week go? Did you do your homework?" Dr. Lewis peered through her glasses at Damon and Audra, eyebrows slightly raised in an expectant expression.

Damon answered. "We did, and it went well. At least I think so." He glanced at Audra and waited for her response.

"I agree."

They rode in separate cars again today, so the first time he saw her was after he arrived. She wore red lipstick and sexy heels, mustard capris, and a polka dot blouse. She smelled good as hell. Not from perfume, but a French lotion she'd fallen in love with. The subtle, flowery fragrance teased him and made his balls ache for a taste of her.

"Excellent." The therapist wrote a note in her book. "What did you talk about?"

Damon shifted his attention to the situation at hand. "The past, the wedding plans for her brother, Ethan."

"He updated me on a new campaign he's doing with Calvin Klein. Oh, and while we ate lunch, we decided to go out again. There's a Children's Cancer Society event we attend every year, and we're going together on Saturday."

The doctor smiled her pleasure. "That's good. Sounds like the conversation went well this time?"

"Yes." Audra turned to him, as if asking him to confirm.

"Definitely better," he agreed with a nod. "Not awkward like before."

"That is very good news," Dr. Lewis said. "I think you're ready for the next exercise. We're going to play a game. This will allow me to see what you think about each other and how well you know each other."

Damon groaned inwardly. A game sounded like a recipe for disaster.

Dr. Lewis laughed. "You both look uneasy, but I promise this could be fun."

She went to her desk and came back with index cards and pens. She handed them each a pen and four cards. Audra flipped hers over, but they were blank on both sides.

The doctor reclaimed her seat. "I'm going to ask some questions, and I want you to write your answer. The person who is not being asked the question will write what you think your spouse did. Write the first thing that comes to mind, without letting each other see the answer. At the end, you'll show me, and each other, what you wrote. Do you understand the rules?"

Audra nodded.

"Sounds like trouble," Damon muttered.

"There are no right or wrong answers. It's simply an exercise for you to see if you're on the same page and for me to get a better understanding of you as a couple. Fair enough?"

They both nodded.

"Excellent." Dr. Lewis crossed her legs.

"Damon, what's the number one non-physical trait you admire in your wife?"

He glanced at Audra, and she glanced at him. What kind of exercise was this?

"Remember, don't think about the answer. You should both write, and don't let your spouse see your answer," Dr. Lewis instructed.

Damon wrote on the card, and Audra wrote on hers. Would their answers match?

"Audra, I have the same question for you. What do you think is Damon's best non-physical attribute? Damon, note what you think her answer will be."

They both finished writing and waited for the doctor.

"Next question. Damon, what is your favorite part of Audra's body?"

They both froze. Damon glanced at Audra, and she glanced at him.

"Write your answers on the index cards please."

Damon did as the doctor asked.

"Audra, what is your favorite part of Damon's body? Damon, what do you think her answer is?"

Easy. He knew that without a second thought.

"Okay, pens down. Thank you. Let's start with Audra, and we'll go backwards. What's your favorite part of your husband's body? Show each other what you wrote."

Damon smiled when he saw the matching answer, and so did Audra.

"You both wrote his back. What do you like about your husband's back, Audra?"

"It's broad and... muscular." She lowered her gaze, almost bashful with the answer.

"She likes to lie on my back." Damon couldn't help the faint smirk lifting one corner of his mouth.

"Is that right?" Dr. Lewis asked.

"And ride on his back," Audra added. "When we were dating, he took me hiking, and—"

"And she didn't tell me she'd never been hiking before," Damon interrupted.

"I was trying to impress you. Not my finest moment." Audra shrugged.

"Halfway up the trail, I thought she would faint. We ended up having to go back before we reached our goal, and I carried her on my back the entire way."

"We never went hiking again," Audra said, shaking her head.

"Shoulda told me the truth," Damon said.

"I said I was trying to impress you."

"How'd that turn out?"

They both chuckled. Damon felt the doctor's gaze on them and returned his attention to her.

"All right, let's continue. What answer did you give for your favorite part of her body, Damon?"

They turned over their cards. Audra wrote butt, he wrote ass. She rolled her eyes.

"Okay, so you like your wife's bottom."

"*Ass*," Damon corrected, emphasizing the word.

"I almost wrote breasts," Audra said.

"Close second." When he dipped his eyes to her bosom, her breath caught.

Dr. Lewis cleared her throat, capturing their attention. "Damon, I won't ask why you like your wife's ass."

His smirk deepened.

"Let's continue, shall we? Audra, what's your favorite of Damon's non-physical traits?"

They turned over their cards. Audra had written that he was a great father, but he'd written his business acumen.

Audra frowned. "You're good at business, but I don't think

that's your best trait. You're a wonderful father and really good with the kids."

"I don't always get things right though."

"You don't have to be perfect. No one is," Audra said.

"What do you like about him as a father?" Dr. Lewis asked.

"He's... good at it. Very attentive. He's playful but knows when to be firm. I tend to hover and worry all the time. In a way, we balance each other out."

Silence encompassed the room as Dr. Lewis wrote in her notebook and Damon digested the words. Hearing Audra compliment his skills as a father was a huge boost to his ego.

"Let's see the last index card," the therapist said.

They turned them over. His favorite of her traits was how she cared for their family. She wrote her sense of style.

Audra frowned. "You're always talking about my sense of style. That's why you had me decorate the house and our vacation properties. You said it made perfect sense that I have a lifestyle blog, and that's why you didn't hesitate to encourage me."

"Sure, but the way you take care of our family and the household is incredible. You know where everything is, you make sure the kids do their homework and help if they need it. You keep us organized and the kids fed. Hell, if it were up to me, they'd eat pizza and chicken fingers every night, but you make sure they have well-balanced meals and encourage Tracy to eat food she wouldn't normally. That's no easy feat."

"You help."

"You do most of the work, though."

Silence fell on the room again.

Finally, the doctor spoke. "Thank you both for doing this little exercise. Your answers were informative, and I want you to notice a theme. Regarding your physical attributes, you know each other very well. With your non-physical attributes, you both talked about the children. Audra, you stated what a great father Damon is, and he stated what a great job you do taking care of the family. At the moment, you see each other as parents. But that wasn't always the case, was it?"

The rhetorical question remained unanswered in the room.

"When was the last time you dressed for each other? When you went on that date the first week, were you concerned about how your spouse viewed you? Or were you simply going through the motions? Think about all of that before our next session, and here's your homework assignment. When you go to the Children's Cancer Society event, wear something your spouse enjoys seeing you in. Audra, I want you to dress for Damon, and Damon, I want you to dress for Audra. When you return next week, tell me what you chose and your spouse's reaction. Can you do that?"

"Yes," they both murmured, nodding their heads.

"Excellent."

When it was time to go, Dr. Lewis told them, "I'll see you next week," in a cheery voice before escorting them out the door.

Chapter Twenty-One

Audra clipped in the last weft of hair and fluffed the dark tresses, gently finger-combing them to blend the weave with her own curls. She secured the left side, pinning the hair back from her face, so the strands only spilled onto her breast on the right side.

She assessed her outfit in the full-length mirror in the bedroom. The strapless black dress swept her ankles and sparkled with rhinestones.

"You look pretty, Mommy," Tracy said, jumping up and down on the bed.

"You think so?" Audra turned to examine the back view.

Dress for Damon, Dr. Lewis had said.

She did look rather nice—nicer than she had looked in a long time. She hadn't worn this dress in ages, but Damon liked her in it. Her butt looked firm and round, and the cinched waist emphasized her hourglass figure. A split came right above her knee, showing off her moisturized, newly shaved legs. She wore a full face of makeup, including red lipstick and false lashes.

The last time she'd gotten dressed up like this had been

a year ago, for the same fundraiser she and Damon were attending tonight. She smoothed her hands over her bow-shaped hips and smiled, feeling beautiful, elegant, and sexy.

The bed's springs groaning under the weight of her daughter's jumps made her turn around. "Stop jumping on the bed, baby."

"One more minute," Tracy said without breaking stride.

"I said stop. That's why your father bought you a trampoline."

Tracy stopped jumping and dropped to her knees on the mattress, pouting.

Audra went into her walk-in closet filled with clothes and accessories on shelves and a clothing store-style turnstile rack that contained slacks and skirts. She stood in front of her wig display in the back, with shelves that spanned the entire wall. She eyed the selection of short, long, wavy, straight, and different colored wigs. Should she have gone with one of the blonde ones? Damon liked her in the wavy, asymmetrical blonde bob.

"That one." Tracy had quietly entered and pointed at a long wig with blunt bangs.

"You like that one?"

Her daughter vigorously nodded.

"Hmm... me too, but for this event, I'm going to stick with what I'm wearing now."

Earrings! She almost forgot them.

She unlocked her jewelry drawer and picked a pair of diamond drop earrings, inserting them into her ears as she exited the closet to take another look at her appearance.

Yes, the earrings went well with the dress.

A giggling Tracy came staggering out of the closet with the long wig on her head. "Look at me, Mommy."

The wig sank low on her head, and the bangs fell into her eyes.

"Put my wig back," Audra said, biting back a laugh.

"No." Her daughter grinned up at her.

"Tracy..." Audra moved toward her, and her daughter took off running, giggling as she went. "Tracy!"

Audra ran to the door in time to see her daughter dashing down the hall with the hair streaming behind her. Shaking her head as she laughed, Audra went back into the bedroom and finished getting ready. She donned a pair of strappy gold Giuseppe Zanotti sandals and an 18-karat gold tennis bracelet set with Asscher diamonds—a push gift from Damon after Tracy was born.

She took one more look in the mirror in appreciation of her reflection. Not bad.

She spritzed perfume on her wrists and neck, picked up her clutch, and left the bedroom. Halfway down the stairs to the first floor, Damon came from the direction of the kitchen, sipping on a bottle of San Pellegrino while Junior regaled him with a story. When he saw Audra, Damon's eyes stretched wide, and he came to a full stop. Water dribbled down his chin onto the front of his three-piece suit.

Junior followed his father's eyes and grinned. "Wow! You look pretty, Mommy."

"That's sweet. Thank you, baby." Heart fluttering, Audra gripped the handrail and slowly made her way to the bottom.

"Doesn't she look pretty, Daddy?"

Damon absentmindedly wiped the damp spot on his shirt. "Yes, she does."

"Thank you. You look very nice too," Audra said in a quiet voice.

He continued his conversation with Junior while she openly ogled him.

Damon owned quite a few suits, but this was one of her favorites. The ensemble fit him like a second coat of skin, hugging his shoulders and tapering to his lean waist and hips. Navy with blue pinstripes, he offset the dark color with a white shirt and rust-colored paisley tie with matching handkerchief. The vest was buttoned, but the jacket remained open. He'd gone to the barber earlier and had a fresh haircut and a groomed beard which brought greater attention to his square jaw and sexy full lips.

Her man was handsome, downright bedazzling like a rare, untarnished gem.

The doorbell rang, and Audra blinked, realizing she had been staring at Damon the entire time. He went to open the door and let in Skye, their babysitter for the night.

"Hi!" Her future sister-in-law wore a megawatt smile. "You two look amazing."

"Thank you, and thanks for doing this. We shouldn't be out late," Audra said.

A sulky Kerilyn dragged her feet into the foyer. "Hi, Skye."

"Hi. What's with the pout?"

"She thinks she's old enough to watch her younger siblings on her own," Damon said.

"I don't think she is yet," Audra interjected.

Kerilyn's lips flattened with displeasure.

"We're going to have so much fun together, though." Skye flung an arm across Kerilyn's shoulder and squeezed.

"Auntie Skye, look at me."

They all turned to see Tracy at the top of the staircase with Audra's wig on her head.

Kerilyn had explained to Tracy once that Skye would become their aunt when she married their Uncle Ethan, so Tracy made a preemptive strike and started calling her Auntie Skye.

"Take that off your head before you come down the stairs," Audra said.

Grinning, Tracy held the handrail and proceeded down the staircase as if her mother hadn't spoken.

"Tracy, do what Mommy said. Take that wig off." Damon spoke in his stern voice, which immediately got their daughter's attention. She tossed the wig onto the stairs and continued to descend.

Audra sighed at the sight of her expensive wig being discarded like a piece of trash. Funny how she had to yell and plead to get the little ones to do anything, but all he had to do was speak the words and they complied.

"I'll put it away for you later," Skye whispered.

"Thank you," Audra said gratefully.

When Tracy reached the bottom, she ran over to Skye and hugged her waist.

Skye hugged her back. "Hey, pretty girl. You ready to have fun tonight?"

"Yep!"

"I guess that's our cue to get out of here," Damon said.

"Call if you need anything," Audra told Skye.

"I doubt I will." Skye always said that in response to Audra's statement.

Nonetheless, Audra went through a list of reminders and told her about the instructions on the island in the kitchen.

"We'll be fine. You two go and have a good time," Skye said.

She shot a look at Audra, perhaps recalling the conversation from their trip to Miami. Audra had explained to her that this was an annual charity event, and they remained in counseling, but Skye expressed her optimism that it was a positive change.

"See you all later," Audra said.

"Bye-bye." The younger kids waved.

Audra walked ahead of Damon into the kitchen, and they exited into the garage. They climbed into his Range Rover, and he backed out of the driveway.

Taking a deep breath, she crossed one leg over the other. "Well, I guess we're on our way," she said, breaking the silence.

"I'm sure we'll have a good time, like we have in the past." The garage door slowly lowered in front of them.

Audra folded her hands in her lap and stared out the windshield. They didn't talk much on the drive to the venue, soft jazz filling the space left by the lack of conversation. Despite not talking, the normal tension she experienced when forced to spend time with Damon alone had thinned.

When they arrived at their destination, he pulled the SUV to a stop in front of the hotel, and a valet came around to the driver's side. They stepped out, walked into the foyer, and signs told them where the event was taking place.

They walked side by side on the way to the designated ballroom, and twice their hands brushed, causing a prickling sensation to skitter up Audra's arm. Her heart raced from the contact, and when Damon took her hand, her racing heart exploded from the electric pulse that ripped through her veins.

Damon stopped outside the door. "Let's have a good time tonight, all right?"

"All right," Audra whispered.

She enjoyed the slightly rough texture of his palm from his woodwork hobby. She hoped this wouldn't be the last time he held her like this. They had agreed to six weeks before making a decision, but if they somehow failed, she would miss the gentle but firm clasp of his hand.

She would miss it for the rest of her life.

Chapter Twenty-Two

Audra was different tonight, moving with an air of confidence Damon hadn't seen in a while. In this mode, she had transformed into the woman who originally caught his eye years ago.

Sexy. Sultry. Smelling good, with the lush scent of roses and orange blossoms in her skin. The entire time in the SUV, he gripped the steering wheel with more force than necessary and fought the urge to place a hand at the back of her neck and pull her onto his lap.

As he let her walk ahead of him so they could wind between the tables, his eyes enjoyed the back view, dropping to the concave arc of her waist and the fullness of her ass in a dress that left nothing to the imagination. Her bare shoulders and the split tortured him. He idly fantasized about her on his lap, while he grabbed her cheeks and let her ride him to oblivion.

Then of course, there was the way she moved. Some women walked. His wife strutted. And he couldn't take his eyes off her.

The gentle hum of conversation filled his ears from guests sitting at the round tables or standing around talking. Much as he appreciated the opportunity to give back, he preferred the events where he could give back in a more active way, such as running a marathon or volunteering to serve food or hand out clothes. But the truth was, these types of fundraisers were also very beneficial. They raised tons of money, keeping the lights on in offices that provided assistance to philanthropic endeavors he and Audra gladly supported over the years.

He caught sight of Elsa Finch in conversation with an older man. When she saw them, she excused herself and came their way. Her shimmering silver dress made her gray hair appear whiter. With diamonds in her ears, she looked like a million bucks.

"Hey you two, so good to see you," she gushed.

They exchanged pleasantries for a moment before she steered them toward the table she and Simon had purchased. "The dinner menu is outstanding this year."

"I didn't eat a bite, so I'll have plenty of room," Audra said.

Damon snorted at her declaration.

Both women shot glances over their shoulders at him with a quizzical expression.

"She rarely eats all her food," he explained to Elsa.

"Is that true? I've never noticed."

"It's not true," Audra said defensively.

"I'm her personal garbage disposal."

Most times they ate out, she ordered more than she could eat, and he had to finish her food, or they took home the leftovers.

Audra shot him a dark look. "Don't listen to him."

Elsa laughed at them.

"Look who's here," she sang as they arrived at the table.

Simon stood immediately. Seeing them together, the

fifteen-year age difference was noticeable. They introduced Audra and Damon to the other guests at the table, which included a couple of attorneys from Simon's firm with their spouses and another married couple who were friends.

In the middle of the casual conversation of getting to know each other, a woman in an evening dress walked on stage and tapped the microphone. The din of conversation died, and the entire room gave her their undivided attention.

"Can everyone take a seat, please? Dinner is about to be served, and then we'll begin the program."

They all sat around a table covered in a white tablecloth with a cluster of lit candles in the middle on a mirrored tray. For the next couple of hours, they ate delicious food, drank wine, and listened to a spate of presenters talk about the various cancers afflicting children and the work they did to not only find a cure, but provide comfort and solace to the young patients and their families living with the disease.

The night's emcee, the same woman who had requested the guests have a seat, closed out the festivities to a round of applause.

Elsa leaned toward Audra but spoke to both she and Damon. "Do you have to rush home? Simon and I are going to the hotel bar after this. Are you free to join us?"

Audra glanced at Damon.

"Sure," he said.

"Good." Elsa smiled her appreciation and then straightened in the chair.

They said their goodbyes, and the two couples strolled through the lobby to the bar, where they sat at a square table. Simon opened a tab, and they ordered drinks.

During the conversation, the waiter returned and placed their drinks in front of them.

Audra pulled her Long Island Iced Tea closer. "How did the two of you meet?"

Damon sipped his vodka and cranberry juice. Despite knowing Simon for years, he didn't know the answer to that question.

Elsa glanced at her husband, a smile touching the corners of her mouth. "Purely by chance."

"Fate interceded, or I could have had a very different life. Not nearly as interesting, I'm sure," Simon said.

Elsa placed a hand on his thigh. "He's quite the charmer, isn't he? Would you believe we met when he was on his way to a blind date with another woman?"

"No way," Audra said.

"Absolutely true," Simon said. "A friend set me up on a blind date with his girlfriend's friend. The plan was to have a low-pressure date, so my friend and his girlfriend were going to be there at the bowling alley. I arrived earlier than everyone else, and as I entered the building, Elsa was leaving."

"I was with a group of girlfriends, having a little fun on a Saturday night before we went to dinner. I didn't see him because I was busy chatting with my friends."

"But I saw her," Simon interjected.

"Do you know what this man did? He turned around and approached me while I'm talking to my friends."

Simon shrugged. "I couldn't let her get away. I was struck by her beauty, by her presence."

Elsa blushed. "He took me completely by surprise. Of course, I had no idea he was there to meet another woman. Initially, I thought, 'This man is too young for me,' but for some reason, I gave him my number."

"What about the date?" Damon asked, enthralled by the story.

"I went on the date," Simon answered. "It would've been

rude to abandon my friend and the women we were supposed to meet. Afterward, I told the other woman—I no longer remember her name—that I enjoyed myself, but I didn't think we were a good match. She didn't seem offended. She agreed, and I never saw her again."

"Which left you free to pursue Elsa," Audra concluded.

"Yes."

"How did the two of you meet?" Elsa asked, her eyes bright with interest.

"I know this story," Simon said.

"Let *them* tell it," Elsa teased.

Damon and Audra glanced at each other.

"At a party," Damon replied.

"A friend dragged me to the party, insisting I needed to get out. She was right, of course. At the time, I hadn't been dating a lot because I had my daughter, Kerilyn. Her father wasn't around much, and she kept me busy most of the time, so going to the party was a big deal. I almost didn't go because of all the celebrities expected to be there, and my daughter's father was in the public eye. All the men I had dated since were not, on purpose."

"Less pressure," Elsa guessed.

"Yes, and more time to spend with family," Audra answered.

"Family is very important to you," Elsa guessed.

"Yes."

Audra's voice thickened, and the emotion echoed in Damon's chest. They synched perfectly in that regard.

"The party was at my condo, and the moment I saw her, I wanted to meet her," Damon added.

He saw beauty, friendliness, and a bit of haughty indifference to the raucous laughter and flirting around her. He'd been more than interested. He'd been downright smitten from one look. Not only by her appearance, but she exhibited a certain aura that drew him in.

"I told the other men to steer clear of her. She was mine."

Audra stared at him in shock. "You called dibs on me?"

Damon laughed. "When you put it that way, I guess that's what I did. I called dibs on you." He ached to touch her right then. "But she didn't know who I was."

"You had no idea he was the famous baseball player—Damon 'The Flash' Foster?" Elsa asked with a delightful laugh that indicated she relished this bit of information.

"I'd vaguely heard his name before, but I didn't pay attention to baseball."

"Unlike you, she didn't give me her number," Damon said to Simon.

The other couple laughed.

"After I found out where she worked—at her stepfather's company—I sent flowers and gifts, but nothing broke her down. She refused to go out with me."

"Why did you give him such a hard time?" Elsa asked.

"After the party, I researched him, and he had quite a reputation with the ladies. I assumed women came easy to him, and if he was really interested, he would stick around and stay the course. I figured that not giving in would be a challenge to a man like him, who was used to getting everything he wanted when he wanted."

It was Damon's turn to stare in shock. "You played me?"

Simon chuckled. "Uh-oh, the truth comes out."

"Nothing wrong with us women having our secrets." Elsa winked at Audra.

Chapter Twenty-Three

After over an hour of conversation, Simon asked for the check and wrote his signature on the receipt with a flourish.

"Thank you, sir. Y'all have a good night," the waiter said before he disappeared.

The couples exited the bar and went to the valet stand outside the hotel.

"I hope we didn't keep you too late," Elsa said. "I know you have little ones at home."

Audra waved away her concern. "It's fine. Our babysitter is my future sister-in-law, and I sent her a text before we went into the bar to let her know we'll be later than expected. She doesn't mind. She loves spending time with the kids."

"That's nice. I remember those days of having to get a babysitter for a night out."

The Finches had twin sons in college.

"You're wise to give yourself time away from your children," Simon added. "We didn't always."

Elsa let out a rueful laugh. "We love our boys, but the

biggest mistake we made was making them the center of our world."

Simon nodded his agreement, slipping an arm around his wife's shoulders, making Audra aware that she and Damon stood side by side—close but not touching.

"We had a rough patch in our marriage, and Elsa dragged me to counseling."

She nodded. "Kicking and screaming."

They both laughed.

Elsa continued. "We learned to make time for each other, apart from our sons, and our counselor pointed out we didn't have much of a marriage anymore because our whole lives revolved around *them*. Every major decision we made was contingent on how it affected the boys. Can you believe that?"

Audra smiled briefly. Her friend's words hit home.

Elsa shook her head, as if she couldn't accept what a major mistake she and Simon had made. "We love our boys, but we had to learn that we were not married to them. We were married to each other, and one of the best things we could do was present a united, happy front to our children. Not only as an example for their relationships but to salvage ours."

"We started dating again," Simon interjected. "The more time we spent together alone, without the pressure of kids and the business, the more we learned about each other. We fell in love again, and lucky for us, we made the change early on, before it was too late."

"Counseling saved our marriage." Elsa spoke to Damon and Audra, but her eyes remained on Simon.

"Thank goodness she made me go. As you know, she's the smart one in the relationship."

"Stop," Elsa said, though clearly pleased.

He rubbed her shoulder, and their loving gazes locked on each other.

Audra envied their closeness. She and Damon might as well be an ocean away, which exacerbated the longing.

"This is us," Simon said, as a yellow Lamborghini rolled to a stop in front of them.

"This is the one, huh?" Damon said.

"This is my girl," Simon said, voice filled with pride.

Elsa let out an exaggerated sigh. "Men and their toys. It was good to see you both. We need to get together again real soon."

The men shook hands while the women hugged.

Elsa slipped into the passenger seat, and Simon hustled around to the driver side. After they drove away, Audra and Damon stood silently beside each other, both in their own thoughts.

Listening to the Finches discuss how they'd neglected their marriage for their children was sobering. Was that part of the problem with her and Damon?

When the valet pulled up in the SUV, Damon opened the door for Audra, and within seconds, they were on their way home.

"It was good seeing Simon and Elsa," Audra remarked.

"Yeah, I always like when we get together."

She smiled, eyes on the road ahead. They made small talk about the event until they arrived at the house and found Skye in the den watching TV.

"How was your night?" she asked, switching off the television.

"Very nice. Delicious food, and the strides they've made in cancer research blows my mind. The organization raised millions of dollars, and we had good conversations with our friends and their guests. How were the kids?" Audra asked.

"Wonderful, as always. I spent most of my time with Junior and Tracy. We played games and watched *Zootopia*."

"Again?"

"How many times have they seen the movie?" Skye asked.

"At least a dozen."

Skye laughed. "Well, they enjoyed themselves and didn't give me any trouble when I told them it was time to go to bed."

"Thanks for watching them for us."

"We really appreciate it," Damon said.

"No trouble at all. You know I love those babies." Skye picked up her purse.

"I'll walk you out," Damon offered.

Skye and Audra said goodbye to each other, and Skye left out the front door with Damon.

Audra climbed to the master bedroom and stripped out of her clothes, donning pajama shorts and the matching spaghetti strapped top.

She removed the hair pieces, washed her face, and brushed her hair before climbing into bed. Lying in the dark, she stared up at the ceiling. Elsa and Simon seemed so happy. They touched each other with obvious affection, love, and ease, their teasing glances filling her with envy.

Therapy had really opened her eyes, and a lot of thoughts went through her head as she lay alone in the California king —a bed way too big for one person. She sorely missed talking to Damon. He didn't say much, but he listened, which she appreciated. And he laughed at her jokes, including the corny ones.

It saddened her that he didn't know what a great father he was. Had she been skimpy with praise?

Almost forty minutes later, she hadn't fallen asleep.

Wired from the drinks, conversation, and her own thoughts, she pulled on her slippers and silk robe and walked into the quiet hallway. The lights were off under all the doors.

In the kitchen, she opened the snacks cabinet and peered up at the shelf. Something crunchy and salty should work. *Oh, we have salt and vinegar chips left,* she thought with excitement.

She stretched onto her toes, elongating her body to reach as far as she could, but she wasn't tall enough. She swore softly. Being short really sucked sometimes. She should climb up on the counter. The idea made her giggle, and she decided she would, despite having chairs she could use only steps away.

Pushing upward, she swung one knee onto the counter.

"What are you doing?" Damon stood in the doorway.

Embarrassed, Audra dropped onto her feet. "Getting a bag of chips."

He looked lethally handsome in only pajamas and his chest bare. Curly hairs were sprinkled across his pecs and abs down toward the tempting vee revealed by the low-slung pants.

Audra swallowed to wet her parched throat.

He strolled to where she stood. "Which one?"

"The salt and vinegar chips."

Inwardly quaking, she held her breath as Damon came to stand in front of her. He crowded her in the corner before she could move and reached above her head to the shelf. Audra pressed against the counter, and the smooth edge cut into her back.

He pulled down the bag. "Anything else?"

He didn't step away, so she had an up close and personal view of his tight abs covered in a sheet of chocolate. She wanted to lick him.

"No, thanks."

He walked to the refrigerator, and with the distance, she breathed easier.

Damon poured a glass of water. "You need me to put those back?"

"No, I'm fine." This was a take-the-whole-bag-upstairs kind of night.

She lingered unnecessarily.

"I figured you'd be asleep by now. What are you doing up?" He grasped the glass in one hand, long fingers curled around it the way they used to curl around her throat as he growled his passion and sliced into her with deep strokes.

"I couldn't sleep. What are *you* doing up?"

"Thinking." Seconds lapsed. "About us."

Same as her. "What were you thinking about?" Audra asked in a low voice.

He released a humorless laugh. "Everything. The difference between our marriage and Elsa and Simon's."

"There's a huge difference. The counselor they were talking about is the same one we're going to?"

"Yeah."

As Damon returned the container of water to the refrigerator, Audra's eyes remained glued to his tattooed back. Immense longing filled her. Her husband stood only feet away, and she didn't feel as if she had the right to touch him.

"What happened to us?" she whispered.

He faced her with bleak eyes. "You know what happened."

"Don't assume, remember?" she said, reminding him of the lesson they learned in Dr. Lewis's office.

"Right." Splaying his fingers on the island, he glanced sideways at her. "I think it was the miscarriages. They..." He shook his head, unable to continue.

Audra's face crumbled and she nodded, choked up.

"I didn't mean to upset you," he said.

"It's okay." She took a tremulous breath. "You're right. That was the beginning of the end for us. It was slow. Gradual. Like a snowball rolling downhill, the rift between us became wider over time."

Damon came to where she stood and used two fingers to angle her chin higher. "Did I fuck up?"

His touch lifted the air from her lungs, his warm fingers inflicting heat on her skin. She almost crumbled at his feet.

"I think we both did."

"I'm sorry if I wasn't there for you. If I didn't give you what you needed."

He seemed inclined to take the bulk of the blame, but she couldn't allow him to do that. A marriage was made up of two people, and they both needed to put forth an effort to make their relationship work.

"I'm sorry too. I'm so sorry." Her voice cracked with the tears that filled her throat.

Damon pulled her into his embrace, and she wrapped her arms around his waist. It felt good to nestle against him and receive comfort. Breasts flattened against his chest, her nipples tightened at the contact.

"Damon..."

"Yes?" His voice, low and husky in her ear, caused tongues of heat to lick at her skin. She was full on aroused. Her insides clenched, brittle nerves shattering from the wear and tear of the past seven months.

Her hands coasted over his warm skin, and he let out a soft moan, grabbing big handfuls of her ass.

"Baby," he breathed. The single word sounded like a plea.

With the long fingers of one hand clenched on her butt, Damon used the other to tug her head back and slant his mouth over hers. He kissed her hard, ravaging her lips and practically devouring her whole.

Audra strained toward him on her toes as their tongues twisted and twirled around each other. She moaned at the delicious taste of him. Her husband. Her lover. Her heart. Her forever.

She had missed the intimacy and explosive chemistry she'd only ever experienced with him. Cradling the fullness of one breast in his hand, he squeezed and dragged his thumb across the tight peak beneath the robe's silky material.

As his mouth trailed down the side of her neck with open-mouthed kisses, she kept her head tilted back to fully indulge in the heady sensation of his lips touching her skin. He hadn't touched her like this in so long, she shuddered as if thrown naked into Arctic air.

"Damon..."

"Shit, baby, I'm sorry," he rasped in an apologetic voice, lifting his head.

"No, don't stop."

Audra grabbed the elastic waistband of his pants. She didn't want to sleep alone tonight. The touching and compliments earlier in the evening had affected her. Tightly wound, she longed for him to untwist the chord of need in her body.

Cupping his hair-roughened jaw with one hand, she gazed into his eyes. "Come to bed with me. Please."

Chapter Twenty-Four

Audra stripped out of her robe and nightclothes and stood naked beside the bed in front of Damon.

"Fucking gorgeous," he said, his husky voice frayed with hunger.

"Now you," she said quietly.

She strutted over to where he stood and hooked her thumbs in the waistband of his pants. Slowly, she pushed the garment down his hips to his ankles, revealing powerful thighs and a rock-hard erection. As she slowly rose to her feet, she dragged her tongue from the base of his shaft to the tip. His chest heaved with a deep inhale, his whole body tense as he watched her intently and took the licking.

Damon kicked his feet out of the pants and lifted Audra in his arms like she weighed no more than an armful of feathers. He marched to the bed and pulled her down on top of him with his back against the pillows.

She took a moment to simply enjoy the sensation of their connected bodies—skin to skin, soft on top of hard.

With his long fingers flat against her spine, Damon kept

their bodies together as he dragged his tongue along her lower lip. Audra's stomach clenched tight, fingers curling into the soft sheets. He tugged her lip between his teeth, sucking on the soft skin until she emitted a moan of frustration and grabbed his face to take control. A needy, hungry, devouring kiss ensued.

Having him beneath her was like a return to the gates of heaven. She opened to his demanding tongue and rotated her hips against his rock-hard flesh.

Smoothing her hands over his beautiful body, she slowly made love to him with tender kisses on his throat and along his collarbone. She teased his hard nipples, first pinching with her fingers and then laving with her tongue. He let out a sound of pleasure—a deep grunt of male content that encouraged her to continue.

Using openmouthed kisses, Audra tasted his skin with the excitement of a new lover. He was salty yet sweet—a deliciously complex mix she had always savored.

Tenderly, she stroked his hardness with her fingers, relishing the smooth, hard texture of his full erection. She eased between his legs and dragged her teeth along the inside of his thighs. Turned on by his scent, she locked eyes with him and kissed the head, then flicked the sensitive frenulum, satisfied when his fingers tightened to fists at his hips. She moved to the veined underside, playfully teasing with the tip of her tongue. The tender kisses left him immobile, his abs tense as he watched her perform for him.

Finally, with a saucy smile, she tugged him into her mouth. She sucked with enthusiastic pulls and slurps, pretending his dick was the most delicious popsicle and she needed to gobble it up before it melted in the sun.

With an audible gasp, Damon's body arched off the bed. "Ah fuck, baby. *Goddamn.*"

His penis throbbed and precum leaked into her mouth, so

she focused harder on bringing him to completion. Pulling him farther into her mouth, she loudly moaned because he liked to hear her enjoying the task.

His low, satisfied groans were her reward, and so were his fingers, which abandoned the bed and curled into her loose hair. Their clasp on her scalp tightened, and his undulating hips conveyed how much he enjoyed her mouth.

Audra knew when he was about to come because Damon had a tell. His right knee bent slightly to fight off the pending orgasm, but he was no match for the swirl of tension building in his loins.

She took him deeper still and played with his balls, watching as his knee bent toward the ceiling at a deeper angle. Finally, he relinquished the fight and gave in to the orgasmic waves that pummeled him.

He released a loud groan that twisted his face into a grimace. His lean muscles tightened, and his magnificent body shuddered. Throat arched, another loud groan escaped his lips, followed by a stream of curse words that he muttered to the ceiling as his pumping hips accelerated the spill of his essence into her mouth.

The hand at the back of her head gripped hard for several seconds before he let go—his body deflated, drained of strength in the aftermath. Audra swallowed every drop of her husband's cum before releasing his limp penis and watching him take ragged breaths to regain control.

"Come here," Damon rasped.

She took her time crawling up the bed and straddled his torso. "You called?" she whispered.

His answer was to pull her down and pluck a dusky nipple in his mouth. She gasped as fiery need lanced through her. She was already hot and aroused from giving him head, so it didn't take much to crank up the heat.

Braced above him, she trembled as he licked her sensitive nipples and bathed her breasts with the precise strokes of his tongue. The peaks contracted to the point of aching, and additional moisture flooded her core.

Damon opened his mouth wide and took in more of her soft flesh, as if eating ripe fruit straight from the branch of a tree. While he sucked one breast, the thumb of his right hand rubbed the nipple of the other. The relentless drag of his rough finger caused her to tremble and plead with him for reprieve.

He muttered something unintelligible and slid his hand higher until his fingers circled her throat. Gently, he eased her onto her back and ground his hips into her aching sex.

"I think we need to open the toy box."

With his hand around her neck, she could barely control her excitement.

"Yes," she hissed.

"I'll pick."

Audra waited against the pillows while he went to the armoire and unlocked the toy box. He returned to the bed dangling the fur-lined handcuffs and nipple clamps with a beaded silver chain in his hands.

She immediately stretched her arms above her head in anticipation.

"Why're you so anxious?" Damon teased. He sank onto the bed.

"I'm not," Audra denied, but she didn't drop her arms.

Damon opened a section of their specially made headboard and revealed a hidden compartment. He released a chained hook, affixed the handcuffs, and then clamped them around her wrists.

With a satisfied smile, he lowered his head. One by one he kissed her breasts, rolling his tongue around her engorged nipples, which prompted her back to curl off the bed. When he

177

was done torturing them, he secured the padded end of a nipple clamp around her left breast. Sliding the binding ring higher, he tightened the toy to the exact pressure she enjoyed. After almost nine years of marriage, he was very familiar with her pain threshold, and the intense pinching made her gasp and her toes curl.

"Ready for the next one?" he asked softly.

"Yes," she replied in a trembling whisper.

"Say please."

"*Please*," Audra begged.

She swiped her tongue between her lips and waited with bated breath for him to apply the other. He didn't right away, of course, because he loved to torment her. He squeezed her breast, massaging and caressing until she twisted in agony with soft whimpering cries.

Finally, he latched the second clamp to her nipple, and her eyes rolled back in her head. She suffered from sensory over-load—at his mercy with her hands cuffed above her head, the cold beads of the chain, and the stimulating pressure of the clamps on her breasts.

And now Damon was working his way down her body. "Been so long, I forgot how you taste."

Audra spread her legs in a wanton display of need, and his soft laughter whispered against the flesh right below her navel. He kissed lower and then his tongue—*oh goodness*—his tongue swept against her clit. It wouldn't be long now. Whenever he went down on her, she quickly exploded.

His beard gently scraped the inside of her thighs. Opening his mouth over her tender flesh, he teased between her legs with slow, deliberate licks, whispering words of praise and promises of carnal deeds to come.

When he pulled the bundle of nerves between his lips and sucked, the climax hit like a speeding locomotive. Fast, hard, unstoppable. She could barely stand to look at his dark head between her thighs. Her body convulsed, and her head tossed back as passion devoured her whole. Husky cries filled the room as he continued to eat her with bestial fervor—lapping at her damp skin, refusing to allow one drop of honey to escape his mouth. He was relentless. Taking obvious delight in her complete loss of control.

The mattress shifted when Damon settled on his knees between her legs. Leaning over her, he tugged the chain connecting the clamps. Audra grimaced at the intensified pinch on her nipples.

"Slow or fast, baby?" His dark eyes glittered above her.

Audra could barely think after such an intense orgasm. "Slow," she answered breathlessly.

She wanted to savor every stroke and every touch because it had been so long.

Damon plucked one, then the other clamp off her nipples. Blood rushed to the tips of her breasts, making the skin extra sensitive to touch. He stroked his tongue over the peaks and grazed them with his teeth. Barely able to stand much more of his demanding mouth, her head thrashing from side to side, and her whimpering mewls filled the room. But the sounds of protest fell on deaf ears. He took his time and didn't stop until he was satisfied, almost giving her another orgasm from such provocative torture alone.

Cradling her bottom, Damon guided her hips into his. Her breaths came in short, fast spurts. She needed him so much.

With a swift, smooth thrust, he took possession of her, and her aroused body absorbed him with ease. Hard nestled into soft and wet. They fit together perfectly. Always had.

Their bodies moved in a sensual rhythm—slow and steady, just as she'd asked for.

Sinking her teeth into her bottom lip, she dug her heels into the bed and pushed off the mattress each time. She shared her desires in hoarse whispers, begging Damon not to stop and pleading to the heavens for aid against the onslaught of pleasure.

"I love seeing you like this," he breathed. Eyes darkened and nostrils flaring, he pinned his gaze on her jiggling breasts. "You feel so good, baby, I'm not gonna last long."

He lowered his lips to her neck and with a gentle suck the fine tremors of an orgasm coursed through her body and intensified with each measured pump of his hips.

Helpless against his thrusts, she let out a loud whimper. "*Damon...*"

"Right here. I got you."

Once again, she lost control. Legs shaking, fingers bunched into fists as she tugged against her restraints. She loved the sensation of powerlessness the cuffs provided but hated that she couldn't touch or hold him.

Damon groaned, his big body driving into hers with unrelenting persistence. As she spasmed around him, he rammed into her with deep grunts. His hands gripped her thighs and pried them wider for his manic thrusting.

She bathed him in feminine juices. Their pace became frenzied and her cries incrementally louder. Months of craving had brought them to this point of a throbbing, wildly powerful climax that seemed never-ending.

Until the chorus of their voices slowly died, and they lay exhausted on top of the sheets.

Chapter Twenty-Five

L oud thumping woke up Audra.

"Mommy, open the door!" Tracy yelled.

"Mommy, I'm hungry!" Junior joined in the knocking and yelling.

"What the hell?" Damon grumbled behind Audra. The arm around her waist shifted, and his hand slid lower to cup her hip.

"Those are your children," Audra said, her words muffled by the pillow.

"They're always my kids when they act up, huh?"

"Mhmm."

"What time is it?"

She blindly stretched for her phone and knocked over a bottle of lubricant in the process, bringing back memories that made her ass throb. Last night, Damon had reclaimed every part of her with no-holds-barred intensity.

"You're doing great, baby," he had whispered, his voice hoarse and rough. "Your ass was made to take my dick."

Audra peered through the tangled hair that covered half

her face. "After eight," she mumbled. She returned the phone to the table with a sigh.

The doorknob wiggled aggressively.

"When did you lock the door?" she asked, twisting onto her back with a low moan.

The delicious soreness of good sex dominated the nooks and curves of her body. Her inner thighs ached, and her nipples were sore from his persistent sucking. She felt desired and sexy, languorous and more than satisfied. Sated.

Damon sat up and yawned. Running a hand down his face, he blinked into the sunlight. "Last night, after you fell asleep. I figured one or both of them would barge in here since it's the weekend."

Ever since they stopped sleeping in the same bed, sometimes Junior and Tracy came in and joined her. A few times, they'd slept in the bed with her, something Damon didn't allow after they passed the toddler stage.

"The door is locked. We don't lock doors in this house," Tracy shouted in an annoyed voice.

"I wonder where she got that from?" Damon pondered with an amused expression.

"You know where she got that from. Me. Go get your daughter before I choke her out on this fine Sunday morning."

Damon chuckled as he slid off the bed, and her chest tightened at the beautiful sound—a sound which had been sorely missed.

"I don't want to be a party to murder," he said.

Her eyes locked on the fineness of his physique framed by the light coming in the window as he bent and lifted his clothes off the floor. His firm glutes and muscular back were a sight to behold, and a tingle of arousal fluttered in her breasts and between her legs from simply looking at him.

More knocking, this time not accompanied with yelling. Her children were certainly persistent.

Damon glanced at her as he trudged toward the door, his smile lazy, his gaze slumberous.

Gosh, he was sexy.

Audra pulled the covers up to her neck. "I'm going to get a little more sleep."

"You don't want breakfast?" he asked, hand on the doorknob.

"No, just make sure they eat."

He swung open the door, and the pounding came to an abrupt stop. She couldn't see Junior and Tracy but imagined them staring up in shock at the sight of their father instead of her.

"Do the two of you pay bills up in here?" he asked.

No response.

"Do you, Tracy?" he asked.

"No," her daughter replied in a soft voice.

"Do you?"

"No," Junior responded, equally meek.

"Then you have no business making all that noise so early in the morning," Damon continued in the same stern voice.

"But where's Mommy?" Junior asked.

"Asleep, but all that knocking might wake her up, and she needs her rest. She had a very long, rough night. She's exhausted and worn out in a way she hasn't been in months."

He did not have to say all that. Audra bit her bottom lip, fighting back laughter. Her arrogant, full-of-himself husband had returned.

"What do y'all want for breakfast?" Damon asked as he stepped out.

The closed door muffled the rest of the conversation as they moved down the hall.

Closing her eyes, Audra couldn't help but smile. Last night signaled a shift, and she was excited to see what would happen next. They had made love and slept in the same bed. At the very least, they'd have to put the divorce on indefinite hold.

* * *

Audra removed the chicken breasts from the oven and set the sheet on top of the stove. When they cooled, she'd add them to the big salad in the fridge, which she'd prepared for her and Damon's dinner.

Damon strolled into the kitchen in burgundy basketball shorts and a gray V-neck T-shirt.

"Dinner almost ready?" he asked, peeping over her shoulder as she cut a piece of chicken.

"Yes." She tasted the meat. "Hmm. Does this need more salt to you?" She fed him from the fork she used.

"Tastes good to me. Not as good as you though." He palmed her bottom and nipped her neck.

"Would you..." Audra glared at him with fake anger.

"I'ma behave." His hands slid up to her breasts and gave a quick squeeze.

"Damon!" She smacked him with the dish towel, and he staggered back, laughing.

"I'm good now. That'll hold me until later."

"Later?" Audra repeated.

"Uh-huh."

"What's going to happen later?" she asked, resting a hand on her hip.

"We're going to reconvene in the bedroom."

"Is that right?"

"Trust me. I know what I'm talking about."

She laughed, going to the fridge to get the ingredients to make the honey mustard dressing. "You're pretty confident."

"Yes, I am." Damon walked out the kitchen with extra swagger in his step.

Earlier in the day, Monica had come by and picked up Tracy, Junior, and Kerilyn to spend the afternoon with her working in the garden since Rose was away on vacation. Audra had run errands and returned home to find Damon and Zack enjoying burgers in the den while they watched ESPN.

After Zack left, she expected her and Damon might struggle with conversation, but last night's connection flowed into today, and they watched a movie on the sofa, snuggled together like old times.

If anyone were to ask how her marriage fared, she'd say they were in a much better place compared to a month ago. Yet an undercurrent of something missing wouldn't allow her mind to settle. The feeling created a knot of trepidation in her chest, signaling issues between them remained unresolved.

She wouldn't dwell on those thoughts at the moment. For now, she wanted to enjoy every minute of relaxed ease she and Damon were experiencing. By his teasing, that meant more sex, and she ached for the slide of his body into hers again.

"I talked to Simon while you were out and told him things were better between us. I thanked him for suggesting Dr. Lewis." Damon lazily played with a lock of her hair.

Settled under Damon's arm, Audra curled her legs beside her. She'd missed the touching and simple act of being in each other's company.

"What did he say?"

"After the Children's Cancer Society event, he had wanted to ask about our relationship but didn't want to pry unless I was ready to talk."

Audra lifted her head. "Are we going to continue going to therapy?"

"I think we should. It's been helpful so far, right?"

"Definitely."

He didn't take his eyes from hers.

"What?" Audra said.

"You looked so damn sexy in that dress last night, and you smelled good. All I could think about was getting you into bed."

He cupped the back of her head and drew her closer. He kissed each corner of her mouth and withdrew to look into her eyes.

Audra got the impression that he was seeking permission, making sure she wanted the kiss. Hesitation was not a word she would have associated with her husband, so she leaned in and kissed him full on the mouth to make sure there was no misunderstanding.

They moved gently at first, and the tip of his tongue playfully pushed at the seam of her lips. She melted into him and opened her mouth to take in the pink snake, which immediately stroked against her own tongue.

Damon cupped her cheeks and deepened the kiss. Curling her arms around his strong neck, Audra swung one leg over his thighs and felt his erection against her abdomen. His thumb brushed her breast, and the ache of desire flooded her core.

Damon's mouth teased her jawline and the curve of her neck, while under her shirt, his fingers wreaked havoc up and down her spine. His fingers were magic. He knew how to touch and where and how much pressure to apply.

He found her mouth again, this time kissing harder. Whatever he did, she enjoyed.

Audra reached her hand into his shorts and slid her hand along his smooth, hard flesh. Damon cursed, his grip on her back momentarily tightening.

"Do you like that?" she whispered.

"You know I—"

The jarring sound of the doorbell caused them to freeze.

Reluctantly, Audra tried to ease away from Damon, but he refused to let her go, his arms tightening around her waist and his lips returning to the side of her neck.

"Ignore it," he whispered.

The doorbell sounded again, and Audra pushed against his chest. "I can't. It might be Monica and the kids. She said she'd be bringing them back around this time."

Damon swore, pulling his rumpled T-shirt over the bulge in his pants and flopping his head against the back of the sofa.

Audra straightened her clothes and hurried into the foyer. Sure enough, she saw her family outside and opened the door.

"Did you forget your key?" Audra asked Kerilyn.

"Yes," her eldest answered.

Tracy and Junior rushed inside with an excited, "Hi, Mommy! Look what we have." They showed her the small boxes they each carried filled with corn, cucumbers, okra, and tomatoes.

"Wow, that's a lot of vegetables."

"We did all the work," Junior said.

"Why doesn't that surprise me?" Audra teased her sister.

"Wow, thanks for ratting me out, Junior. And they didn't do *all* the work. I helped a little bit." Monica showed Audra the additional bounty of vegetables in a paper sack. "Can you use all of these?"

"We sure can. Thanks." She took the bag. "Are you coming in?"

"No, I'm going home."

They all said goodbye, and Audra watched her sister climb into her other vehicle, a white Porsche Cayenne, and pull away from the house. She went into the kitchen, where she found the boxes of vegetables on the floor. Junior and Tracy were on the carpet in the den watching TV. Damon reclined on the sofa. Kerilyn had already disappeared upstairs.

Audra found space for the vegetables and then joined her family in front of the television. Hours later, she told Junior and Tracy it was time for bed.

"Can we stay up a little bit longer? Five more minutes," Tracy said.

"Yeah, five more minutes," Junior agreed, holding up five fingers.

"You two always want five more minutes. It's past your bedtime. Turn off the TV and let's go upstairs. Bath time and then to bed."

They both moaned but turned off the television and dragged out of the room.

Damon stood, and she recognized the sheen of lust in his eyes.

"We need to finish our conversation," he said.

"Is that what we were doing? Talking?"

He came to stand directly in front of her, a towering specimen of pure male making her tilt back her head to gaze up at him.

"Our bodies were talking."

"I guess we can finish our conversation after I put Junior and Tracy to bed?" Audra suggested.

"Sounds like a plan."

"Give me forty-five minutes."

He nodded, and she left the den.

By the time Junior and Tracy were in their pajamas and had climbed into their beds on opposite sides of the room, most of the time had already elapsed.

After tucking them in and giving each a kiss good night, Audra turned out the light and slipped from the room. Despite their groaning and carrying on, they'd be asleep within minutes.

She rushed into the master bedroom, stripped out of her clothes, and hopped in the shower. Afterward, she brushed her hair into shiny sheets onto her shoulders.

She pulled her silk robe over a baby doll nightie she hadn't worn in forever so she wouldn't seem overly anxious. Then she sat on the bed and waited, heart racing. Had forty-five minutes passed yet? She hadn't checked the time.

Two soft knocks on the door, and Damon slipped in. Her heart beat faster, and she stood to face him.

He only wore pajama bottoms, and she immediately knew he'd taken a shower like she did because the fresh scent of pine soap greeted her nostrils.

He ambled over and loosened the knotted belt on her robe to reveal the nightie underneath.

With a brief head shake, he pulled his bottom lip between his teeth. "You're so damn sexy. Gonna be another long night."

"I can handle whatever you dish out."

Damon bent his head, lips insistent on the swell of her breasts, his tongue dragging with lewd intent toward her hard nipple.

Audra closed her eyes, her mouth fell open, and she gave herself over to the sensual magic of his touch.

Chapter Twenty-Six

"I have a better one," Audra said as they stepped on the elevator on the way to their weekly counseling session.

"Oh, no," Damon said with an exaggerated groan.

Audra had told him a terrible joke and threatened him with another one.

"This one is good, I promise."

He eyed her with blatant skepticism. Today she looked sexy as hell in a short-sleeved dress, green with white flowers and a ruffled hem. The neckline dipped low over her generous bosom, revealing her tantalizing cleavage. How did he get so lucky?

"Go ahead."

She straightened her shoulders as if about to give an important speech. "What do rich clouds do?"

He already knew the joke was going to suck. "What do rich clouds do?" he repeated, screwing up his face.

"Yes, what do they do?" She clasped her hands together, bursting to give him the punchline.

"Tell me."

"They make it rain." She burst out laughing.

Her smile brightened his day. His heart went crazy, and he let out a little laugh. Man, he'd missed seeing such unbridled happiness in her.

"That joke was terrible," Damon said.

"It was fantastic. Come on, tell the truth."

The elevator doors opened, and they stepped out.

"My wife, the comedian, ladies and gentleman," Damon announced, with a mocking sweep of his hand to the empty hallway.

Audra angled her head higher and curtsied.

"You have no shame," he told her.

"And you're dishonest. That joke was hilarious."

"Maybe a little funny. A tiny bit." He held his forefinger and thumb close together.

"*Hilarious*," Audra insisted, cutting her eyes.

He opened the door to the therapist's office, and she waltzed in ahead of him.

Minutes later, they were still disagreeing and teasing each other when the receptionist escorted them into the counseling office. At her desk, Dr. Lewis glanced up from the computer.

Audra covered her mouth with her hand. "Excuse us."

The therapist rose from her chair, notebook and pen in hand, wearing a simple black skirt and white blouse. She sat across from them. "Don't apologize. The sound of laughter is the sound of happiness, and I like my clients to be happy. Please, catch me up on what's happened since we saw each other last. Start with the fundraiser."

Damon let Audra take the lead in recounting how they dressed for each other and what happened at the event, interjecting every so often with additional details. They also told her about the renewed sexual intimacy between them.

Dr. Lewis finished writing her notes. "Well, you've had

quite a week."

They both laughed, seated closer to each other than when they started the sessions. They'd also ridden over in Damon's Range Rover instead of driving separately.

"It seems the act of dressing up for each other and going out worked better this time?"

"Definitely," Audra said.

"All right, let's dive into some of what you told me. Damon, you admitted to warning other men away from Audra at your party that day. Why did you do that? You didn't know her."

"I didn't need to know her. I sensed she was special and wanted to be with her. I didn't want anyone else to mess up my chances." He didn't regret his actions. "Don't forget she played me by pretending not to be interested."

Audra's mouth fell open. "I didn't play you."

"That's what it sounded like to me. I tried to talk to you, and you ignored me even though you were interested. Had me acting like a stalker sending gifts and flowers and shit to your job."

"You were just used to having your way with women and getting anything you wanted."

"A spoiled jock," he guessed.

"You said that, I didn't," she pointed out.

Truth be told, he had been spoiled, with lots of money and women at his disposal.

These counseling sessions had benefited him in another way. They taught him to be introspective, and he gained a better understanding of his past behavior. Sleeping around with all those women had been a form of self-medication, so he didn't have to dwell on his childhood abuse and its ramifications. He used women as an escape, not unlike the same way an addict might use drugs. Meeting Audra changed his life.

"Did you have any concerns when Damon continued to

shower you with gifts even though you didn't express interest?"
Dr. Lewis asked Audra.

"No, but Benicio, my stepfather, had concerns. He wanted
to know who this man was and asked if I wanted him to get
involved."

"What was he going to do? Break my legs?" Damon asked
with some amusement, though he'd probably offer the same
services for his daughters.

"*No*. Maybe give you a stern talking to."

"Wouldn't have worked. I was obsessed."

She lowered her gaze, a faint smile of pleasure coming to
her lips. He reveled in the fact that he could still make her
blush.

"What did you tell your stepfather?" Dr. Lewis asked.

"I told him that I didn't want him to interfere."

"Why not?"

Her eyes dropped and so did her voice, becoming lower,
softer. "I liked the attention."

Damon made a mental note of that. On a surface level, he
understood how paying attention to his wife made her feel
good, but hearing her say the words made him determined to
shower her with attention. Making her happy became his new
priority.

"You mentioned your friends, the Finches," Dr. Lewis said,
"and how the conversation with them helped you better understand how you were focusing on your children to the detriment
of your marriage. I've seen that often with clients. There's
usually a cause and effect in these situations. The effect is, you
withdrew from each other and focused on your children. Any
idea what caused the change?"

The room became silent, and the light-heartedness disappeared. The stillness in Audra ripped his heart to shreds, and
Damon took the lead this time.

"We, uh, had a few miscarriages. Three over a two-year period. The last one occurred about eight or nine months ago. They took a toll."

"I'm sorry," Dr. Lewis said, her eyes compassionate.

Audra's lips tightened, and Damon took her hand, satisfied when some of the tension eased from her shoulders.

She glanced at him before she spoke. "Losing our pregnancies caused us to change. We didn't realize it at the time, but gradually over a couple of years, we grew further apart, and we hurt each other. One of the hardest parts for me was when Damon didn't..."

Damon seized on the unfinished sentence. "I didn't what?"

She withdrew her hand from his. "You didn't want me anymore." The words came out in a barely audible whisper.

"That's what you thought?" Damon asked.

Audra continued to avoid eye contact. "That's what I know. You became so different from the man I married."

"What did I do to make you think that?" He turned his body in her direction, ready to accept any incoming blows.

She faced him. "It wasn't one thing, Damon."

"Then tell me one of the things."

"You stopped buying me flowers," she whispered. "You used to buy me flowers all the time."

He couldn't deny he used to do that. That was their thing. He'd bring home flowers, and she'd act surprised, as though it was the first time.

She continued. "It's not the flowers per se..."

"I know. The thought. What else?" he asked.

"Dr. Lewis, I don't think we should do this."

"Don't talk to her, talk to me," Damon said, getting aggravated.

"We're in a good place. I don't want you to think I'm attacking you," Audra said.

"I'm a big boy. I can take whatever you have to say. What else?" he demanded, almost angrily.

Audra licked her lips, and her eyes turned glassy with tears. "Why dredge up old anger and feelings?"

"Cause and effect, Audra," Dr. Lewis gently reminded her. "We need to talk about these things, get them out in the open so you can both understand what happened and why, so it doesn't happen again."

They were in a better place now, and he understood why Audra didn't want to speak her mind because she was sweet-natured and worried about hurting him. But he agreed with the doctor. They needed to understand every aspect of their relationship.

"Y-you stopped paying me compliments, and you obviously didn't want me anymore because you stopped touching me."

"That's not why I stopped touching you. It's because every time I did, I could tell you didn't *want* me to touch you. You recoiled—often."

"I admit that sometimes I didn't want to be touched, but not often," Audra said.

"Sometimes, often, all the time—it's all the same to me. My wife didn't want me to touch her, and I understood at first. We had lost another baby, but when you kept pushing me away and started faking your orgasms..."

Her mouth fell open. "How did you—"

"I knew." He knew her body, probably better than she did. He knew when her body was pleading for more of him, and that had stopped.

"Not for the reason you think. I stayed in my head. Every time we had sex, I kept thinking about getting pregnant, which reminded me of..." Her voice faltered. "It wasn't you. It was me."

"I thought you didn't want me anymore, so I pulled back," Damon admitted.

"I thought you pulled back because you were no longer interested. You hardly ever slept in the bed with me anymore."

"Sleeping in the guest room was easier than getting rejected all the time," Damon admitted.

"You weren't upset or maybe disappointed?"

"Disappointed?"

"That we couldn't have more children."

"I was disappointed, Audra, but I didn't blame you, if that's what you think."

"You wanted a big family, and so did I." She wrapped her arms around her torso. "You did your part. You bought the house to accommodate a large family. You left baseball, so you could be an involved father. I had one job." Her lower lip trembled.

"Stop." He pulled her into his arms. He'd had no idea she'd been beating herself up about the miscarriages. How many times had the doctors explained there was nothing she could have done?

"It's no more your fault than it is mine," he said quietly, hands gentle as they smoothed up and down her back.

She cried, releasing all the pain and guilt she'd been holding on to.

Dr. Lewis rose from her chair and came back with a box of tissues. Damon pulled out two and handed them to Audra.

She dabbed at her eyes. "I'm sorry."

"Don't be," Dr. Lewis said. "This is a breakthrough session. We—the three of us—better understand the root of the problem. What caused you to pull away from each other, what caused you to focus more on your children. When you love someone, truly love them, you make yourself vulnerable to the ravages of pain. When the pain strikes, the agony is intense, and after a while, good sense dictates that you escape rather than endure such devastation, similar to our natural fight-or-flight response when we encounter danger. You both retreated to your corners to avoid pain from the person you love. Based on what we've uncovered in these sessions, I believe you still love each other, and you're closer now than when you started counseling weeks ago. With your permission, I'd like to end this week's session early. Is that okay?"

They both nodded.

Audra reached for Damon's hand, and he threaded their fingers together, holding on tight.

"Excellent. As usual, I have a homework assignment for you. Two parts. First, I want you to go on another date, alone this time. The Children's Cancer Society event was a good start, but you were with other couples. Dress up again, but this time spend time alone. Second, I want you to focus on the positive aspects of your partner, to help your relationship thrive. Our words have power. They can uplift or tear down. I want you to uplift each other and fill your marital well with positive words. You're going to leave what I call love notes for each other. They should be one or two sentences long about what you appreciate or love in each other. You'll leave one a day.

"For instance, Damon, you might write Audra a note stating that she looked lovely in this dress. But don't only focus on the physical. Include compliments about non-physical traits you appreciate in your partner. Audra, you could leave Damon a note letting him know how he comforted you when he held you a few minutes ago. This exercise is to make you think about all the things you love about the person you married. Be romantic, be corny, and make your partner feel appreciated. Positive reinforcement is what we're shooting for." Dr. Lewis paused and smiled at them. "By the way, I'm very happy with your progress. I'll see you next week."

197

Chapter Twenty-Seven

A veritable hotspot in Atlanta, Notte Italian restaurant not only served delicious food, but they also had an intimate vibe. Dark wood walls, dimmed lights, and votive candles flickering on each table gave the impression the establishment was small, despite its large size.

For tonight's outing, Audra wore black slacks, a pink top, and heels, hair framing her face in full curls. Damon opted for black slacks and a gold and black shirt with a black blazer.

They entered the restaurant hand in hand and were soon shown to their table. The waitress arrived, a dark-haired young woman in her early twenties. Her mouth fell open when she recognized Damon.

"Flash," she said, eyes going wide.

Damon smiled. "How are you doing?"

She clutched her chest. "Oh my gosh, I have Damon 'The Flash' Foster at my table. Night made! I'm Lana, and I'm a huge fan. In high school, I used to go to the games with my dad. He had season tickets, and you were our favorite player. The year that you..."

Audra was used to fans approaching Damon—men and women. Some women did the most. Leaning in close and laughing way too hard at his jokes. Sometimes they'd dart a challenging look in her direction. Despite all that, she'd always been secure in their relationship, except when they were struggling. Not anymore.

She perused the menu while Damon politely listened to the woman gush, nodding his head and answering questions. Being his usual charming self.

Finally, he said, "Well, I guess it's our lucky night that my wife and I landed in your section."

"Oh shoot, where are my manners," Lana said. "Hello, Mrs. Flash. Sorry about that. You two wanted to have a nice dinner, and here I am, running my mouth."

"It's okay," Audra said, smiling so the waitress wouldn't think she was upset.

The young woman took a deep breath, as if to calm herself. "What can I get you to drink?"

They placed their orders, including an appetizer of bruschetta to start, and then the young woman left them alone.

Damon rubbed his jaw in a thoughtful way. "I've been thinking about Keri's sixteenth birthday coming up, and I think we should buy her a car. Nothing fancy, but whenever I let her drive, she does a good job. She's careful."

Audra nodded. "I was thinking the same thing. I'm proud of her grades this year, and Ethan said she's doing a really good job. The managers are impressed with her work ethic."

"So, we're in agreement?" He raised an eyebrow.

"Yes. Although my heart will be in my throat every day for months when she first gets that car."

Damon squeezed her hand. "She'll be fine. She's a smart kid."

"I know, but it's hard to loosen the reins. I'm trying."

"It'll get easier."

Audra nodded. "Oh, by the way, the roof on the property in the DR is fixed. Maybe we should go down there in the fall—for a few days—since we didn't get a chance to visit during spring break like we had planned?"

"I like that idea."

With flexibility in both their schedules, they could easily travel when they needed to. They both knew the reason they hadn't gone in the spring was because of their strained relationship. Now Audra looked forward to fun in the sun at their beachfront property. All three of their kids were adventurous, and the last time they went, they all five came back with darker skin and lots of memories from snorkeling trips, a visit to a cluster of waterfalls, and eating delicious seafood dishes which included fish they caught when Damon rented a catamaran with a local guide.

Dinner lasted over an hour, and they spent the meal tossing out ideas about the kind of car they could purchase for Kerilyn, settled on a date for the trip to Arkansas to see Damon's parents, and covered a myriad of personal and business-related topics. Damon ended up eating part of Audra's lasagna and finishing her order of tiramisu, and before they left the restaurant, he signed a page in Lana's notepad.

Instead of heading home, they went for a walk to take advantage of having time away from the kids, who were spending the night at her mother's.

"Did you ever think we would be like this again?" Audra asked.

"I had serious doubts," Damon admitted.

"I hated when we fought, and I missed you when you didn't join me at family events."

"I fell off," he said. "When we were struggling, I didn't

want to be around your family and pretend everything was fine. Not when I was miserable."

Audra understood.

"We should have never gotten to the point where we wanted to divorce," he continued. "We made a vow to stay together in sickness and in health."

"For richer or poorer," Audra murmured.

"As long as we both shall live," they finished.

"Nothing's changed for me," Audra said. "I feel the same way I did when we married."

"So do I." Damon stopped walking and edged them out of the way of pedestrian traffic. He pressed her back against the wall of a building and leaned over her. "There ain't nothing out there for me. Everything I want is at 7205 Lakeland Crossing."

"You want more kids," Audra pointed out.

For so long, she held on to the guilt of not giving him what she'd promised. Their six-bedroom house should be filled with children and their laughter. She felt guilty, as if he left baseball and bought a big house for nothing.

"We already have kids," Damon responded.

"But you want more. You grew up an only child and wanted a big family, and I understand. I had two siblings and then four more. I grew up in a chaotic house with five brothers and a sister and family always visiting from Georgia, out-of-state, or Mexico. I wanted that for us—for you. I wanted to give that to you."

"We have three beautiful, energetic children who keep us on our toes. I'm not greedy. Truth is, if we didn't have any children at all, I'd still be happy. You're all I need. *You* have always been the center of my universe. Not the kids, and I lost sight of that."

"So did I," Audra admitted quietly.

"I married you, and I'm going to spend the rest of my life

with you. When Keri, Junior, and Tracy, are gone and have their own lives, we'll be left alone together. We need to work on us. We need to keep making our marriage a priority."

"I agree." Audra paused. "If you don't necessarily want more children, do you mind if we stop trying? It's... hard. I-I don't want to go through that again." Her voice wavered as her throat closed.

Damon cupped her face. "I know. I saw your struggle, and after a while, I wondered if I was hurting you when we kept trying. But I thought that's what you wanted."

"I did want to keep trying, but like you said, we have three beautiful children. I'm happy. They'll have to be enough."

"Tell you what, since we're not going to have more kids, I'll talk to a doctor about a vasectomy."

Her eyebrows lifted in surprise. "Really?"

"Yes."

"You're not worried about..."

"What? My masculinity?" Damon snorted. "I don't worry about that foolishness. Getting a vasectomy don't have nothing to do with how much of a man I am."

She allowed a smile to spread across her face. "I'm so lucky."

"Me too. Luckiest man in the world. Other men want what I have, but I'm not letting none of those sneaky bastards slip between us and take away my bad bitch."

Audra laughed.

"What? You don't think you're a bad bitch?"

"I don't know, I..."

"You're a bad bitch."

She laughed again.

"I'm serious. Say it."

Audra rolled her eyes. "I'm a bad bitch," she muttered.

"Say it like you mean it. Loud and proud."

"I'm a bad bitch!" she yelled.

A couple walking by stared at them, and she ducked her head, mortified.

"That's right," Damon said, unperturbed by the attention. He lifted her head with a finger under her chin. "What else can I do for you today?"

"I wish we could've had a wedding. You know, with our families present. Unfortunately, we can't travel back in time."

"How about we have a huge anniversary party next year, for our tenth?"

"Oh, that would be perfect. I'd love that."

"That's what we'll do."

Audra suddenly had an idea. "Why don't we adopt?"

His lips parted as the idea registered. "We could do that. Hell, I'm adopted. Why didn't we think of this before?"

"Because we were concentrating on having biological children, but now that's off the table, adoption would be a great way to expand our family."

Excitement lit up his eyes. "Yes! Let's adopt."

Audra wrapped her arms around his torso and gazed up at him. "We can have another baby! Babies."

He chuckled, joy breaking his face into a broad grin. "We can."

"Ready to head back?"

"I am."

As they started in the direction they came from, Audra winced because her feet hurt.

"What's wrong?" Damon asked.

"These heels. I shouldn't have agreed to go for a walk with you. They're not exactly the most comfortable shoes that I own."

"Oh, I see what you're doing," Damon said, slowing to a stop.

"What am I doing?"

"Hint, hint. Get on."

"I wasn't trying to hint that I want a piggyback ride, Damon."

"Sure you weren't. Go ahead."

"Damon."

"Audra."

They had a stare off.

"Get on my back. You know you want to."

"I don't."

"I'm going to count to three, and if you don't get on my back, you'll have to walk the rest of the way on hurt feet. One—"

"Okay! I'm not going to be stubborn. My feet really hurt."

He bent his knees, and she climbed onto his back, giggling as she wrapped her arms around his neck.

"You good?" he asked, hooking his arms around her legs.

"Mhmm."

Damon started the trek back, and an older couple eyed them.

"Way to take care of your lady, young king," the man said as they passed, his voice filled with approval.

Damon chuckled, and Audra grinned the entire trip to the parking lot.

When they reached the Range Rover, he lowered her to the ground with a sigh. "My work is never done. I have to eat your food, and I have to carry you to the car on my back."

"As you should," Audra said. "You heard that man. You're supposed to take care of me. If you're a king, I'm a queen. Your queen."

"Yes, you are." He opened the door, and with a sweeping hand gesture said, "Your chariot awaits."

Audra didn't climb into the vehicle. She grasped his blazer

and pulled him closer, gazing up into his eyes, chest filled with emotion.

He rested his forehead against hers. "I know, baby."

"We almost gave up." A tear leaked from the corner of her right eye, and she wiped it away. "I swear I'm crying all the time lately."

He enclosed her in a warm hug. "We're gonna be okay. I promise."

For the first time in a long time, she believed that to be true, but the road to getting here had been long and arduous. Audra rested her cheek against Damon's chest.

Slowly, she moved her hand around to the front of his pants and undid his belt buckle.

Damon stilled—his body and his breathing.

"What are you doing?" he asked in a hoarse voice.

She gazed up at him with a flirty smile and let her working hands be the answer.

He pressed his face into her neck and scraped his teeth along the line of her throat. "Let's go home."

"I want to stay here. Let's get in the back seat."

Spontaneous sex outside of the bedroom, something they hadn't done in ages, thrilled the blood in her veins.

She didn't have to tell him twice. They climbed into the back of the vehicle and kissed hungrily. She caressed his hard flesh the way he liked, gently massaging his balls and dragging her fingers up the full length of his shaft to the tip. She wrapped her fingers around his length, and he groaned, his breath reduced to short pants.

Audra lowered her head and took him in her mouth, playing with the tip and then sinking low and sucking harder.

"Take all of it," he commanded in a rough voice, placing a hand at the back of her head.

His groans grew louder, and she knew without looking that

his head had fallen back. She knew her power and how he responded to the suction of her mouth.

When she lifted her head, she began unbuttoning her blouse and watched with satisfaction as Damon gazed at her with heavy-lidded, darkened eyes. Impatient at her slow movements, he pushed away her hands and yanked apart both sides of her blouse.

He popped open the front clasp on her bra and pressed his face to her breasts. Her nipples tightened to stiff buds at the sensation of his warm skin and bristly beard. Sighing, she cupped the back of his head to smash him closer.

"Get on this dick," he commanded in a gruff voice, gripping her hips.

Audra shoved off her pants and underwear, and with one hand, he dragged her leg across his thighs and pulled her onto his lap. His hard erection pressed against her belly as their eager kisses increased desire between them.

Without hesitation, she lifted onto her knees and lowered until she was impaled on his rigid length. They both moaned while trying hard to keep quiet so they wouldn't attract attention, but it was darn near impossible to keep down the noise when they were together like this. She tightened her arms around his neck and began to ride, and he helped by pulling her hips into his thrusts.

She controlled the pace for a spell, until Damon swore softly, his voice sounding like a mixture of anger and lust. He scooted his butt toward the edge of the seat to give himself better leverage to pump his hips, while he continued to hold her with strong hands. Audra gripped the back of the seat and closed her eyes, losing herself in the sensation of him plunging repeatedly into her body, while his hands wreaked havoc on her thighs, hips, and bottom.

The sexy dance was uninhibited as they simply enjoyed

each other. She moved faster and strayed toward a pending orgasm, biting her lip to restrain the noise that threatened to burst free.

"I'm coming," she whimpered.

"Go ahead, baby. Let me hear you come," Damon breathed.

He kept time with her, hips moving in tandem, eyes focused on the bounce of her exposed breasts.

She finally came, and her body rocked with an earth-shattering tremor. She let out one guttural cry and then clamped her mouth shut to keep the sound from carrying across the parking lot, before she collapsed in a heap on top of him.

Damon came right after. His big body jerked beneath hers. The grip on her butt cheeks tightened, and his groan came low and heavy as he let loose inside her.

Spent, Audra closed her eyes and rested her forehead on his shoulder.

After a while, Damon shifted and sat up. Audra refused to let him go, her arms remaining encircled around his neck.

"That was so damn good," he said.

She laughed softly. "Yes, it was."

He kissed the corner of her eye, letting his hands lazily run up and down her spine. "We need to do that again sometime."

"Definitely."

She lifted her head. "I love you so much."

He stroked her jaw and placed a tender kiss on her lips. "Love you too, baby."

Chapter Twenty-Eight

"I love Taco Tuesday," Tracy said.

She danced on a stool beside Audra. Her excitement was contagious. Audra laughed, chopping fresh cilantro for the pico de gallo.

"I know you do. Mwah." She smacked her lips, giving her daughter a loud kiss on the cheek, and Tracy giggled.

Audra enjoyed moments like this and wondered if her relationship with Tracy would one day go in the same direction as her strained relationship with Kerilyn. She hoped not. She couldn't bear to experience indifference from both her daughters.

On Taco Tuesdays, Audra created a taco bar and allowed her family to make their own soft or hard tacos, with fixings like pico de gallo, guacamole, lettuce, and cheese. She finished chopping the herb and then scraped it into a bowl with tomatoes from her mother's garden and onions. Then she sprinkled on salt and squeezed in fresh lime juice.

"Stir everything together so the flavors get evenly distributed," she instructed.

As Tracy stirred the vegetables with a spoon, the doorbell rang.

"Keri, would you get the door for me, please," Audra called out, turning the meat on the grill pan.

No answer from her daughter, and the doorbell rang again. Damon and Junior had gone to get haircuts. Knowing her teenager, she probably reclined in her room, FaceTiming with friends or listening to music with her earbuds in.

"Stay away from the stove," Audra warned, heading out the kitchen.

"Okay, Mommy."

The doorbell rang again. "Coming!"

She hustled into the foyer. Opening the door, the sight of a large bouquet greeted her eyes—a gorgeous summer mix of oranges, yellows, and reds. Damon had sent her flowers!

Her spirits immediately lifted. He was thinking about her.

She signed the electronic pad and closed the door. Balancing the bouquet in both hands, she walked into the kitchen and placed it on the island.

Tracy's eyes went wide. "Those are pretty."

"They sure are."

Audra opened the envelope and read the card. *I'd be lost without you.*

Tears filled her eyes.

As instructed by Dr. Lewis, every day they left each other love notes.

Yesterday she slipped one in the duffel bag Damon took to the gym.

You're an amazing father and husband. We're lucky to have you.

He later told her the message filled him with pride and a sense of accomplishment because he'd done what he set out to do, becoming the opposite of his biological father and more like the man who had adopted him. He spent the rest of the morning on a natural high, and Zack had accused him of acting weird.

"Mommy, what's wrong?" Her daughter's curious face locked on her.

Audra stuffed the card back in the envelope. "Oh, nothing."

"Are those from daddy?"

"Yes."

"And they make you want to cry?"

"These are happy tears."

"Oh." Tracy finished stirring the pico de gallo. "All done."

Audra peered inside the bowl.

"Good job."

Tracy jumped off the stool. "Can I watch TV?"

"Sure, baby."

Her daughter skipped over to the den. She flung herself onto the sofa and flicked on the television.

Audra placed the flowers in a prominent spot on the island and went back to cooking. When Damon and Junior arrived, they both had their hair trimmed low. Junior turned in a slow circle to give her the full effect.

Audra cupped his face, so much like his father's. "Don't you look handsome."

"I got a lollipop. Cherry." He stuck out his tongue.

She laughed at his red tongue. "I see."

"The flowers arrived," Damon said with a smile.

"Thank you. They're beautiful." Audra slipped an arm around his waist, and they briefly kissed.

"Mommy was crying," Tracy announced from the sofa, unprovoked.

Damon shot Audra a quizzical look.

"Happy tears because of the flowers and the words you wrote on the card."

"I meant them." He patted her bottom.

Kerilyn strolled in. "Mom, can I go to Kayleigh's house this weekend?"

Damon left the room, and Junior plunked down on the floor to watch TV with his sister.

"Sure. As long as her dad is home. Will he be?"

"Yes." Kerilyn filled her arms with dishes and walked carefully over to the table to start setting it.

Audra eyed her daughter. Kerilyn had gotten better at lying. Not like when she was little and couldn't tell a lie to save her life.

"I hope you're telling me the truth."

Her daughter paused, glancing over her shoulder and looking at Audra without blinking. "I am."

"How are you going to get there?"

"She's coming to pick me up."

"Keri, you know I don't like you riding with other teenagers." To start setting up the taco bar, Audra transferred the meat into a dish on the island.

"She's going to be careful. I promise. She's been driving for months now."

"I'm aware, but I want you to be safe."

"I know, because you don't want me to make the same mistakes you did," Kerilyn said in a tired voice.

Audra placed a spoon in the bowl of guacamole. "The wrong decision can derail your life. I don't tell you these things to make you miserable. You're smart, and you have so much potential. I want the best for you."

"I know, Mom," Kerilyn said in an exhausted voice. "I promise, we're not doing anything that would cause trouble and make you disappointed in me. At some point, you're going to have to trust me."

True enough, she'd done her best to raise her daughter right and given her the tools she needed to make good decisions. Perhaps she should loosen the reins. Just because she'd made terrible mistakes growing up didn't mean Kerilyn would.

"All right, you can go to Kayleigh's. But you have to complete your chores first."

"I will! Can she pick me up?" Kerilyn pressed her hands together like she was about to pray and put on her pleading face.

Audra weakened. "Yes, she can pick you up."

"Yes! Thank you, Mom." Kerilyn rushed over and gave her a hug. "I promise you won't be disappointed. Thank you, thank you, thank you."

Audra smiled. "You're welcome."

That was the closest Kerilyn had come to showing her affection in a while, and she didn't realize how much she needed it until then. She desperately wanted a better relationship with her oldest daughter, but a rift had formed between them ever since Kerilyn hit puberty. They were no longer as close as they used to be, and she missed that. Kerilyn used to spend time with her, but now they fought over the simplest issues.

The relationship with her husband was on the mend, but the one with her daughter needed work.

"Okay, time for dinner," Audra announced. "Junior, go get your father."

While Tracy settled on the bench at the table, Junior moaned and stomped out of the room with exaggerated steps.

"Without the attitude," Audra called after him.

When they were all seated around the table, Damon said grace, and then the kids lined up to make their tacos.

Heart overflowing with happiness, Audra watched her family fix their food and tease each other. She looked forward to discussing the changes during the counseling session in a couple of days.

Chapter Twenty-Nine

"Listen to that," Damon said, carrying a bowl of popcorn from the kitchen to the den.

Audra cocked her head. "What? I don't hear anything."

"Exactly. Silence." He sat down and flung an arm along the back of the sofa behind her.

Snuggling into the crook of his arm, Audra giggled. "It is nice, isn't it?"

During yesterday's therapy session, they recounted the week's activities for Dr. Lewis. Pleased with their progress, she told them weekly meetings were no longer necessary and adjusted the sessions to every two weeks.

"All this is going to change when we adopt," Damon warned.

"I'm ready for the change. We can handle it."

"You ever think about..."

He didn't have to elaborate. Audra nodded, reading his mind. "I wonder about their personalities and how much more chaos we would have in the house if... if they had lived."

He squeezed her closer and kissed her temple. "What are we watching tonight?"

Audra turned on the TV and dipped a hand into the bowl of popcorn resting on his thighs. "I'm in the mood for a mystery or a comedy. Either one is fine."

"Let's watch a comedy. I'd like a good laugh."

"Okay... Let's see what's available."

She checked the comedy category on the app and scrolled through the options, pausing every so often so they could read the synopsis of movies that seemed interesting.

When they finally found one, she clicked start. Damon dimmed the lights, and they settled in to be entertained for the next hour and forty-five minutes. Halfway through the movie, Audra's phone rang.

She reached for it on the coffee table. "It's Keri." It was highly unusual for her daughter to call while she was out. "Hey, baby."

"Mom," Kerilyn whispered.

Immediately on the alert, Audra gripped the phone and sat up straight. "What's wrong?"

As soon as Damon heard the question, he muted the television.

"Mom, please don't be mad at me. I'm not at Kayleigh's house."

"Where are you?"

"I'm not sure. I'm at this boy's house. His name is Barrett, and he's a senior."

Her voice trembled, and Audra's heart lurched.

"Y-you said I could call if I was ever in trouble."

"Absolutely. How did you end up over there?"

"This guy I like—named Jay—me and Kayleigh were over at his house. We hung out there for a while, and then he brought us here. There are four guys here, plus me and

215

Kayleigh. I said I wanted to go home, but Jay—he won't let me. They're drinking, and I don't want to do all of that. I'm scared. What should I do, Mom?"

Audra hopped to her feet. "Are you in a safe place?"

"I'm upstairs in the bathroom. I pretended I had to pee."

"Good girl. Stay there, keep the door locked, and your father and I are going to track you on the app. We'll be right there, okay?"

"Hurry, Mom. Please."

"I'm coming baby. I'm coming."

"What's going on?" Damon asked as soon as she hung up.

Audra rushed from the room, explaining as she went. She grabbed her keys from the rack in the kitchen, but they dropped from her trembling fingers. This was her worst nightmare—that her headstrong daughter would get herself into a dangerous situation. Though she seemed to never listen, she had listened when Audra told her to call if she ever needed help. No matter what the situation, she promised to go get her.

Audra picked up the keys, but Damon snatched them away. "I'm driving." He replaced her keys on the hook and removed his Range Rover keys. "I have the app on my phone, so I'll track her. Call her back and keep her on the phone to make sure she's okay."

Audra nodded, relieved to have his cool, calm personality in this particular instance. Damon thought clearly in frantic situations, whereas she became discombobulated and emotional.

At least the little ones were spending the night at her mother's, so she didn't have to worry about them. They climbed into the SUV and backed out the garage. On the way out the subdivision, Audra's knee bounced restlessly as she tried to reach their daughter again, but Kerilyn wasn't picking up.

"Answer the phone, baby," she said softly. "I shouldn't have hung up. What was I thinking?"

Damon placed a firm hand on her bouncing knee. "She's going to be fine. Try again in another minute. She might've put down her phone."

As soon as he finished the sentence, the phone rang and she answered. "Are you okay?" The question rushed out of Audra's mouth.

"Yes. I didn't answer because Jay was calling for me through the door."

"Do not open the door if you don't feel safe. Do you understand me?" Audra spoke in a slow, firm voice. For her daughter's sake, she needed to keep control of her emotions.

"I told him I was almost finished, and I was coming outside."

"No. You stay right there. Tell him you're sick."

"We're twenty minutes out," Damon said.

"Did you hear that? We're twenty minutes away. We'll be there as soon as we can. We know where you are."

"I'm sorry I lied, Mom. I just wanted to hang out with Jay." Kerilyn's voice cracked and she sniffled.

"It's okay," Audra said in a soothing voice. "I don't care about any of that. I want you to be safe, okay? We're on our way. Stay on the phone with me."

Kerilyn sniffled again. "Okay," she said in a wobbly voice.

About five minutes out, Audra heard banging on the bathroom door and a male voice yelling at her daughter.

"I don't feel good!" Kerilyn screamed.

The male voice said something back to her that Audra couldn't understand.

"Leave me alone! I have diarrhea," Kerilyn hollered.

"That should take care of any problems you have with them trying to come in there," Audra said.

Minutes later, they pulled in front of a large brick house at the end of a cul-de-sac. Because cars filled the driveway, Damon parked on the street, and they hopped out of the SUV.

Audra followed her husband up the stairs to the front door with beveled glass.

"We're here. That's your father ringing the doorbell. You can come out now," Audra said into the phone.

Through the beveled glass, the light came on in the foyer and someone stood on the opposite side looking out at them.

"Who are you?" a young man asked.

"Damon Foster. I'm here to pick up my daughter, Kerilyn."

The young man opened the door. Brown-haired with dark eyes, he frowned at them. Three more boys slowly came from the back.

"Hey, aren't you...?" One of them with dark hair studied Damon.

"Yeah. Damon Foster. Where's my daughter?"

He pushed his way across the threshold, and Audra followed him. She smelled alcohol, though none of the boys held containers in their hands.

Kerilyn came running down the stairs.

"You called your parents?" The brown-haired teen asked, incredulous.

Damon spoke before Kerilyn could. "You got a problem with that?"

The young man fell silent.

Kerilyn ran straight to Audra, who pulled her into a protective embrace. Now that she held her daughter in her arms, she breathed easier.

"Which one of you is Jay?" Damon asked.

The three boys pointed at a tall Black male toward the back. Damon walked slowly toward the young man, who reversed several steps and hit the wall behind him. Puffing out his chest, he hardened his jaw and tilted up his chin, glaring at Damon with a tough guy pose.

Damon stood toe-to-toe with him, almost eye level except he had a couple inches on the teen. "When a girl tells you she wants to go home, you take her home. You don't negotiate. You don't refuse. Because when you do, you know what that's called? False imprisonment."

The young man's eyes widened. "She could have left anytime she wanted."

"What was she supposed to do—walk? She came here with you, genius. But not to worry, because she ain't going nowhere else with you again. Stay the hell away from my daughter, understand? Or I'm coming to see you."

Jay swallowed. "Yes, sir."

They were about to leave when Kerilyn came to a full stop. "What about Kayleigh?"

"Where's Kayleigh?" Damon asked the boys.

One of them pointed into the room behind them, and a young woman with reddish-blonde hair came meekly forward.

"She's staying," the brown-haired boy said. He went to stand beside Kerilyn's friend and placed an arm around her shoulders.

"It's okay, Mr. Foster. I'm staying."

"Nah, that ain't happening. Get your stuff and let's go," Damon said.

"She said she's staying," the boy said.

Damon ignored him and spoke directly to the girl. "Get your stuff. I'm not leaving you here with four boys and alcohol. And I'm going to need you to take your arm off her."

The boy narrowed his eyes, but he dropped his arm. "Who do you think you are?"

"Your worst nightmare if you keep acting up," Damon answered in a matter-of-fact voice. "Let's go, Kayleigh. You can come with us, or I can call your dad and wait until he comes to pick you up. The choice is yours."

"Kayleigh, come on," Kerilyn pleaded.

The girl shot a glance at the brown-haired teen and then back at Damon. "I'll get my stuff," she mumbled.

She went back into the room and returned within seconds with a purse thrown over her shoulder and phone in her hand. She slipped past the group of boys and came to stand with Audra and Kerilyn.

"You boys have a good night," Damon said.

Audra and the girls slipped out the door ahead of him and piled into the vehicle, Kayleigh in the front and Audra in the back with Kerilyn. She looped an arm around her daughter, who rested her head on her shoulder.

"Whose house was that? The brown-haired kid?" Damon asked.

Kayleigh nodded. "His name's Barrett."

"Someone needs to tell his parents what he's been up to," Damon said, reversing.

"It won't matter. Barrett does whatever he wants and gets away with it. His dad's a judge."

"Last year he got into an accident," Kerilyn said. "No one was hurt, but he had been drinking and drove into someone's living room. Nothing happened. He jokes about it."

"Sounds like he's on his way to worse troubles," Damon remarked. "Underage drinking, destroying property, and pretty much doing whatever he wants and knowing there will be no consequences because his parents will get him off the hook."

"Pretty much," Kayleigh said.

"I'm glad you girls are safe," Audra said. "Kayleigh, I'm

going to give you the opportunity to talk to your dad tonight after we drop you off, but I am going to talk to him about this tomorrow."

Kayleigh slumped in the seat. "Yes, ma'am," she said, glum.

Chapter Thirty

Audra scanned the shelves of the open kitchen cabinets and made a note of missing items for the grocery order. She closed the doors and turned around, almost jumping out of her skin when she saw Kerilyn standing on the other side of the island.

She clutched her chest and laughed. "You scared me."

Kerilyn didn't crack a smile. "I figured you wanted to talk to me after last night, so I came to get my punishment."

Audra placed the pen and notepad on the counter. "Your father and I talked, and we're not going to punish you. You've been through enough, and I'm sure you learned your lesson, correct?" Audra raised an eyebrow.

Kerilyn's eyes widened. "I have. You're really not going to punish me?"

"No, because we had an agreement. You can call me any time you're in trouble, and I don't ever want you to hesitate to do that because you're afraid of the consequences. But lying to me and your father is *not* okay, Keri. We need to know where you go when you leave this house. We are responsible for your safety and wellbeing. Do you understand?"

"Yes, Mom."

Audra braced her hands on top of the island. "Furthermore, stay away from boys like Jay. A boy who puts you in a situation like that, who doesn't listen when you say 'No' or 'I'm ready to go' because you're uncomfortable, is not a boy who cares about you."

"I know. I had a bad feeling about going."

"Always trust your gut," Audra said in a gentle tone.

"I will from now on." Kerilyn didn't move.

"Why do you look so sad? Do you want to be punished?" Audra asked in an amused tone.

Her daughter shook her head. "No. I guess I'm surprised, that's all. I figured you'd be all mad."

"I wasn't happy, that's for sure. I don't like that you lied to me, but I worried more about your safety than I was upset, believe me."

"I know I shouldn't have lied," she said softly. "I..."

"What?"

Kerilyn tugged her top lip between her teeth, eyes cast downward, and Audra waited for her to continue.

A lone tear rolled down Kerilyn's cheek, and she rubbed it away with a rough swipe of her hand.

Audra rushed around the island and placed her hands on her daughter's arms. "Baby, what's wrong? Did one of those boys hurt you?" Her stomach tightened in a knot. Damon should have kicked their teenage asses.

"No, they didn't hurt me."

"Then what's wrong? Why are you crying?"

"B-because I screwed up, and now you're going to be even more sorry that you had me."

Audra's head reared back, shocked speechless.

"W-what did you say? What are you talking about?"

Kerilyn sniffled, her shoulders shaking under the weight of her distress. She rubbed her eyes and swallowed.

"Keri, what did you mean by that?" Audra demanded.

"You always say you don't want me to make the s-same mistakes you did, and I figure... I-I'm one of those mistakes. And you wish..." Her voice quivered as she ended the sentence.

Horrified by what her daughter believed, Audra's mouth fell open. She pulled her into a fierce hug, squeezing her tight. "No. Absolutely not. Oh baby, no."

Kerilyn sobbed against her shoulder.

Audra stepped back and clutched her daughter's tear-streaked face.

"My baby, no, no, no. You were not a mistake. Never, ever. Have you been thinking that all along?"

Kerilyn shrugged as she sniffled. "You had me really young, and my real dad never wants to see me."

Audra pulled her into another tight hug, heart hurting because all this time her daughter had believed she didn't want her.

She smoothed her hands over her daughter's hair and pulled back. "Look at me. I want you to get the idea of me not wanting you out of your head right now. Do you understand me?"

Kerilyn nodded vigorously, eyes red and watery, eager to accept the love she thought she'd been denied.

"Do you have any idea how much I love you? I can't even put how much I love you into words." Audra squeezed Kerilyn's arms in a tight grip, as if she could absorb the pain from her daughter's body into hers.

She hated the idea that Kerilyn could believe she was anything like her father. In the beginning, she gave her ex some grace because they were young when they had Kerilyn, and he didn't have a good support system like she did. However, almost sixteen years later, he was worse.

Audra would never forget how he disappointed her for her thirteenth birthday, canceling days before when he'd promised to spend the weekend with her. Damon had saved the day. He rented out an amusement park and threw a huge, last minute birthday party their family and her friends attended. Kerilyn created a collage of photos from that day and framed them, placing them on her bedroom wall where they remained to this day.

"Honey, I'm so sorry. I wasn't thinking when I said those things. I don't want you to have a child at nineteen like I did, but understand me when I say, I never regretted having you. When you were born, I refused to let you out of my sight. Everyone thought I was crazy. I was so protective and hovering all the time. I was worse than I am now, if you can believe it."

Kerilyn gave her a watery smile.

"Friends told me I would spoil you because I was always cuddling you and holding your hand, and hugging you and kissing you. I love being your mommy. Not once did I regret seeing your cute little face smiling at me. I miss that. I miss being able to hug and kiss you. I know you're older now, but maybe you can let me do that sometimes."

Kerilyn sniffed. "I think I can allow it."

"You sure?"

"Yeah."

They both laughed.

Audra swiped the wetness from her daughter's reddened cheeks with her thumbs. "When I talked about the mistakes I made, I was referring to how I ended up in bad situations and got into trouble. One time, a teacher caught me and my friends smoking cigarettes behind the school. Another time, I sneaked out with my friends, and we got into trouble for underage drinking in the park."

"What? *You*?" Kerilyn asked, aghast.

Audra grimaced and nodded. She had been young and dumb. "I was trying to be grown and trying to fit in. Your grandma and *abuelo* were especially livid about the sneaking out and drinking because they did *not* appreciate getting a call from the police."

Kerilyn's eyes widened. "Do you have a record?"

"Thankfully, no. The police took us to the station and called our parents to pick us up."

"Wow. You were lucky."

"Very. I'm not proud of my behavior, but I gave you those examples so you'll understand what I mean when I say I don't want you to make the same mistakes I did. I love you. Very much, and I'm sorry I ever let you think that I didn't want you. Don't ever doubt that. And just like last night, you ever need me, I'm there. You're my baby, and you'll always be my baby. Don't be afraid to call me."

"Thanks, Mom."

Audra hugged her tight and kissed her temple.

* * *

Seated on the cushioned bench on the patio, Audra sipped iced tea in the dark. She'd come outside for a bit of alone time before going up to bed because the conversation with Kerilyn stayed on her mind. She couldn't believe how she'd screwed up her relationship with her own daughter, and the entire time she'd laid the blame at Kerilyn's feet, thinking her daughter was the typical difficult, rebellious teenager.

At least now Kerilyn knew the truth and no longer carried around that hurt. Audra recognized where she had gone wrong.

As Kerilyn matured, she had come down hard on her daughter to protect her, and her actions created a rift between them.

The door creaked open, and Damon stepped out. "I guess you and Keri talked? She seemed in a good mood during dinner."

Audra scooted over on the bench, and he sat beside her, rolling his arm along the back of the chair.

"She's better." Audra launched into an explanation of why they had been butting heads the past couple years.

"You're not going to beat yourself up over this, are you?" Damon asked.

"How can I not? As Dr. Lewis pointed out, words have power, and I was careless with mine." She had not done enough to fill her daughter's well with uplifting words, and because she hadn't been explicit, her daughter had made assumptions about what she meant. She would do better from now on.

"You're human, and being a parent doesn't mean you're perfect. You told me something similar, remember? You didn't know what she was thinking, but now that you do, you can repair your relationship."

"I hate that she ever doubted my love for her," Audra said in a low voice. She set her glass of tea on the table.

Damon squeezed her close. "I'm sure she knows you love her. Want to know how I know?"

"How?" She glanced at him, eager to feel better.

"Because when she was in trouble, she called *you*. She knew she could count on *you*. She knew you'd protect her and keep her safe. Not every parent does that."

He spoke from experience.

Audra soothingly rubbed his thigh and rested her head on his shoulder. "Thanks. I needed to hear that. It'll take a while for me to get over the guilt, I guess."

They sat in silence, listening to the neighborhood sounds. Cars, distant voices, the occasional barking dog.

Damon's fingers trailed along her shoulder. "When we started counseling, Dr. Lewis asked if we would marry each other again." He paused. "If you could marry me again, would you?"

Audra lifted her head. "Yes. I can't believe you asked me that."

His eyes were dark but contained a brightness in the low light.

"In a second," Audra added.

"No question?"

"No question. You're my beginning, my middle, and my end. I want you under my umbrella when the storm comes. I don't want to be with anyone else but you during the rainy days and the sunny days."

He smiled. "That's what I wanted to hear." He pulled out his phone.

Audra frowned. "What are you doing?"

"Hey, Monica, we're good to go." He waited and nodded in response to whatever her sister said on the other line. "Okay. Thanks for your help."

Audra sat away from him. "What's going on? What was that about?"

Damon took her hands in his. "We can't go back in time to have the wedding we should have had, but we can do something else. We can have a vow renewal. You missed out on a ceremony when we got married, and I want you to have a little bit of that ceremony you wanted, when we recommit to each other in front of our family and friends."

"A vow renewal?" Audra repeated, in shock.

"Yes. We can have a big party for our tenth anniversary next year, but this year, let's get married again. We can have a ceremony two weeks from today. Everything's been arranged with the help of a company called Crosby Nuptials. They specialize in vow renewals. We'll take lots of pictures, and you can wear a white dress if you want—or not. You have an appointment at a boutique tomorrow afternoon. A car will pick you up and take you to meet Monica, your mom, and Skye so you can try on dresses."

Her mouth fell open. "What about the kids?"

"I'll take care of them."

"Why are you doing all this?"

"So we can have a fresh start."

Audra loved the idea of a fresh start and climbed on top of him, flinging her arms around his neck. "I love you so much. Whatever you have planned, I know I'll love it."

"Well, I didn't do it by myself, but I do hope you love what we came up with. Because I did it for you. For us," Damon said.

He kissed her then, and their mouths fused together in a passionate caress.

Chapter Thirty-One

T*he best part of my life is you. I can't wait to marry you again.*

The love note Damon left Audra resonated in her head a full hour after finding it in a bag she brought to The Rose Hotel, one of Ethan's properties, which he named after their mother. The vow renewal was taking place in the courtyard, and the reception would take place inside the hotel.

With nervous excitement, Audra did a slow 360 turn, studying her appearance from all angles. "I hope I don't forget my vows," she said to her mother, who sat in a chair nearby.

She and Damon planned to spend a few minutes talking about their relationship and each other before they ended with a recommitment to their marriage.

"You'll do fine," Rose reassured her. "You look lovely, by the way."

She agreed with her mother. The dress, her hair, and her makeup—everything looked spectacular. The elegant design of the dress showed off her figure in a flattering way. Blush-colored and off-the-shoulder, the dress draped to a mermaid hemline into a pool around her feet. She wore her hair in a classic updo with curly tendrils falling on either side of her face.

Skye and her sister entered the room.

"You ready?" Monica asked.

"I'm ready. Why does this feel like it's the first time?"

"Because in a way, it is," Skye said.

There was a soft knock on the door, and the coordinator entered—an amber-skinned woman with a pixie haircut and a pleasant demeanor. "Are you ready?" she asked.

Audra pulled air into her mouth and released it slowly. "I'm ready."

Less than ten minutes later, Tracy led a friend's toddler daughters down the white carpet, the little girls dropping rose petals on the way to the front.

At the back of the venue, Audra waited with Benicio, arm in arm. For most of her life, he'd been her father. She couldn't imagine anyone else escorting her on this special occasion.

"You look beautiful," he said.

"Thank you." She leaned closer, and he kissed her temple.

Two harpists filled the air with the soothing sounds of their instruments. The coordinator and her assistant opened the doors and Audra and Benicio strolled through, beginning the slow walk toward Damon, who looked fine as hell in one of his three-piece suits. Audra could barely contain her smile.

On either side, the happy faces of friends and family greeted her. Claire and Zack and Elsa and Simon were there. Her youngest brother, Maxwell, had arrived from out of town to join the celebration, and Dr. Lewis was in attendance with a satisfied smile on her face. When they reached the end of the aisle, Benicio placed her hand in Damon's, and they went to stand in front of the officiant.

The ceremony was nothing like their first one. Last time,

she was pregnant, nervous, and unsure, wondering if the rush into marriage was a wise one. This time, the renewing of their vows was a joyous occasion. A moment for them to celebrate with friends and family and rededicate themselves to each other.

They agreed beforehand to exchange rings. Her old wedding rings would be turned into other jewelry. Perhaps a bracelet or necklace. When Damon placed the new rings on her finger, she gazed at them in awe though she'd seen them already. Smaller diamonds encircled the bands, but the real star was the halo setting of the engagement ring, with a ten-carat diamond surrounded by round pave diamonds. The set matched beautifully with his new platinum band.

As they recited words of rededication, vowing to honor and love each other, her heart filled with happiness.

At the end of the ceremony, Damon gave her the sweetest kiss filled with the promise of eternal love.

* * *

Damon watched Audra across the room, dancing to a Latin beat with her brother Ignacio. The actor had bound his shoulder-length locs into a ponytail to keep them out of his face as he partied, leading Audra in a series of rapid-fire spins and turns as they burned up the dance floor. The friendliest of her stepbrothers, he had a gregarious personality like his father. Having him take time out of his busy schedule to come to the renewal on such short notice had made Audra very happy.

He fingered the love note in his pants pocket, which she had slipped into his suit at some point the night before. *Your butt looked great in those shorts yesterday. Love you.* The message, written in her slanted, feminine handwriting, had made him smile.

Damon turned to his father. "You all set for us to come see you next week?"

"Oh yes. We have activities planned for almost every day you're in town." He paused. "I'm glad you and Audra were able to work out your problems."

Damon stared at his father. Chadwick Foster was a tall man with a graying beard and round belly. They stood inside the reception hall where guests milled about, and a few couples joined Audra and Ignacio on the dancefloor.

"How did you know we were having problems?"

"Keri called me upset one day. Said you and Audra were getting a divorce."

"You never said anything."

"Neither did you."

Touché.

"How did you fix your problems?" his father asked.

"We went to counseling."

His father raised his eyebrows.

"I know, you're surprised. Believe me, I shocked Audra when I suggested we go. I guess when something is important to you, you do whatever is necessary. That's our counselor over there in the green."

Chadwick followed his line of sight to the therapist chatting with another guest. "She looks young, but I guess she knows what she's doing."

"She's good." Damon paused. "I'm thinking about going to therapy about... about the abuse I lived with as a kid."

"That's a good idea, son."

"I know you and Ma have wanted me to go for a long time."

"You have to want to do it, though. If you're at that point, that's good. We never wanted to force you into going."

"I better understand how talking through what happened to me could help. I've come a long way already, but maybe therapy can help me get past that last block. Sometimes I'm not the best at expressing my thoughts and feelings. Drives Audra crazy."

With the people closest to him, the ones he worried the most about losing, he sometimes seemed aloof. He wanted to work on that.

"She loves you anyway."

"Yeah, I'm lucky. So, since I'm learning to open up more. I wanted you to know how much I appreciate you and Ma. You're a great father. You never gave up on me, no matter how many times I screwed up."

"You weren't always easy," his father said pointedly.

Damon laughed. What an understatement.

He'd been a scared kid when he arrived in their home. Because of his experiences, he never felt completely safe anywhere. For a long time after they adopted him, he kept a trash bag in the back of the closet, filled with clothes he came with. Nothing they had bought him. He'd been prepared for the day when they would send him back.

They never did. He ran away three times. Each time he called, his father came to get him. He'd been testing them. Testing their love. Testing their patience. Would his new father strike out the way his biological father did?

Chadwick Foster never did. Not once. He showered him with love, and that's how he learned to be a patient, loving father to his own children.

"Love shouldn't be conditional, son. You don't give up when it's tested."

"Thank you for adopting me. You saved me," Damon said with heartfelt appreciation. His chest tightened with emotion.

Chadwick grunted. "Don't think it was one-sided. You gave us purpose. Our lives were empty until you came along, and now we have three grandkids in addition." A beatific smile crossed his face. "Our lives are full."

Damon flung an arm across his father's shoulders. "I love you."

"Me too, son." Chadwick blinked rapidly and cleared his throat. With a quick pat on Damon's chest, he straightened. "Let's go find your mother."

* * *

Audra sneaked up on her brother Maxwell and embraced him from behind.

He turned and lifted her off the floor with a bear hug.

"I'm so glad you came," she said, laughing.

A blend of Rose and Benicio, her brother had curly hair, toasty brown skin, and a beard.

"I didn't get to see you get married, so I had to come to this celebration."

"When do you go back?"

"Day after tomorrow."

"Wow, they gave you two whole days off."

He chuckled. "No one was more shocked than me."

"Mom's happy?"

He nodded, rolling his eyes but looking pleased, none-theless. "She's spoiling me."

"Of course. Her baby's home."

"So, what do you think about our parents and that vacation they took?" Maxwell quirked an eyebrow.

"You talked to Monica?"

"Yeah."

"I wish I knew what happened on that trip. According to Monica, when she tried to get information out of Mom, she wasn't forthcoming. All she would say is that she and Benicio are in a better place."

"Monica told me the same thing. They got along fine before, so what does that *mean*—a better place?"

Audra shrugged. "Only time will tell."

A strong arm slipped around her waist from behind, and Damon's unique scent filled her nostrils.

"Mind if I steal my wife for a dance?" he asked.

"Not at all," Maxwell replied.

Damon led her in front of the DJ, who played Kenny Lattimore's "For You." They slow danced together, gazing into each other's eyes.

"I'm happy we did this," he said.

"You sound surprised," Audra teased.

"Not surprised, but I didn't realize how much I'd enjoy it and how much I'd missed by not having a regular ceremony with our friends and family present to celebrate with us. We should do this again but a smaller ceremony next time. Maybe you, me, and the kids."

She lifted her eyebrows in surprise. "That's so romantic. When?"

"How about year twenty?" he suggested.

Audra tightened her arms around his neck. "I *love* that idea."

"Then that's what we'll do." He bent his head and gently kissed her.

The DJ turned on the "Cha Cha Slide," and a roar of groans mixed with laughter went up from the group. Family and friends poured onto the dance floor and lined up in rows.

Damon danced sandwiched between Audra's Aunt Florence and her mother, Rose, with Tracy and Junior bouncing around in front of him, screwing up the steps but having a blast. To his far left, Audra shook her sexy ass between

Maxwell and one of her cousins. The entire group danced together until the song ended.

They partied until late into the night when the little ones fell asleep on their grandmothers, the men clustered together smoking cigars, and an exhausted Audra relaxed in a chair with her head on Damon's shoulder.

Chapter Thirty-Two

Junior halted in front of the island and sniffed. "What's burning?"

"Nothing. Mind your business." Kerilyn slid the last pancake onto a stack on a yellow platter.

"Did you burn the pancakes?" he asked.

"I said mind your business."

"You burned the pancakes, you burned the pancakes," he sang, pointing his finger and wiggling his butt.

"I burned one," Kerilyn snapped. "You know what, no pancakes for you. You get on my nerves!"

"Keri, don't talk to your brother like that," Audra said, taking the glass pitcher of orange juice to the table.

"But he *does* get on my nerves. He's so annoying."

"He's little. Junior, behave and stop harassing your sister."

An unrepentant Junior smirked and sauntered to his seat at the table.

Tracy dashed into the kitchen, knocking into her sister, who carried the platter of pancakes. Kerilyn staggered backward, holding the stack high to balance them and keep them from falling.

"Oops. Sorry," Tracy said, wide-eyed.

"Why are you guys always running everywhere?" Kerilyn demanded.

Audra refrained from reminding her daughter she used to have the same bad habit.

Tracy ran over to the table and sat on the bench.

"Could we please have a nice, quiet breakfast? Thank you." Audra shook her head.

"Mommy, sit next to me, please." Tracy scooted over and patted the bench beside her.

"One second."

Audra brought over the other dishes, and Junior danced in his seat when he saw the sausage and scrambled eggs.

Damon entered the kitchen at that moment and joined them at the table. "This looks good."

"I made the pancakes," Kerilyn said proudly.

"She burned one, that's why it smells in here," Junior volunteered.

"Junior!" Kerilyn and Audra said at the same time.

"Junior, that's enough," Damon said.

His son ducked his head.

Audra and Kerilyn settled on their seats.

"Can I say the prayer this morning, Daddy?" Junior asked.

"Sure. We ready?"

"Oh, I forgot the maple syrup in the microwave." Audra made to get up.

"I got it, baby." Damon jumped up, removed the syrup, and came back to the table with the glass dispenser. "Junior, you're up."

They all bowed their heads.

"Good food, good meat, good God, let's eat. Amen."

Audra opened her eyes and lifted her head. Kerilyn snorted and started laughing, while Damon shook his head. Junior calmly speared a pancake with his fork and moved it to his plate.

"Where did you hear that?" Audra asked.

"YouTube," Junior answered.

"Talk to him," Audra said to her husband, who rested his mouth on his fist to hide his amusement.

Damon placed a couple sausages on his plate. "Junior, that was a good start, but we need to fine tune your skills a little bit. I'm going to teach you how to say grace properly, okay?"

"Okay, Daddy."

"I only want pancakes. Two," Tracy announced.

"Okay, two pancakes for you." Audra placed them on her daughter's plate.

"You need to expand your palate," Junior said, with a mouthful of sausage.

"Where did you learn the word palate? Did you pick that up on YouTube?" Kerilyn asked.

"That's what Uncle Bruno always says. Expand your palate."

"That does sound like something he'd say," Audra agreed, spooning scrambled eggs onto her own plate.

"My palate is fine, thank you," Tracy sassed.

"You don't even know what it is," Junior said.

"Neither do you. So be quiet and eat your breakfast," Damon said.

Audra smiled as she watched her family eat together. Being loud. Being funny. Being loving. She hadn't fully enjoyed these crazy moments when all was not well with them.

She glanced at Damon, and he winked at her. She knew he felt the inner contentment the same as she did.

Tonight was date night, which had been added to the

calendar twice a month on Fridays. She and Damon agreed to take turns planning the evenings out.

Tonight was his turn to plan the activity, and she was excited to see what he had in store for them.

* * *

Audra double checked her appearance in the full-length mirror. At Damon's request, she wore the wavy, asymmetrical blonde wig. Her long sleeve dress had a high neckline with the back scooped low, inches above her bottom. Thanks to the miracle of boob tape, her large breasts sat high and perky despite not wearing a bra. Black heels and large earrings completed the outfit.

"You look pretty, Mommy," Tracy said.

She lay on her stomach on the bed, her scissoring feet bouncing off the mattress one after the other.

"Thank you." She smiled at her daughter through the mirror. She *felt* pretty.

She and Damon were on their way to a nice dinner and then a comedy show in Cobb County.

"I guess I'm ready." Audra turned away from the mirror.

"One second." Keri, who had been sitting in one of the chairs by the fireplace, approached. She repositioned a few strands of the bob and then stood back. "Better."

The improvement in their relationship made Audra immensely happy.

Damon entered from his closet, adjusting a cuff. When he saw Audra, he whistled, one eyebrow lifting higher as delight filled his eyes.

He took her by the hand and turned her in a slow circle and whistled again. "Look at your mom, girls. She looks stunning, don't she?"

Her cheeks heated, and she almost felt the same as when they had first started dating.

"Would you stop? You're embarrassing me," she said, though she loved the attention.

He grinned at her, his eyes filled with promise, and for a split second, she forgot their children were in the room.

"You look great, Dad," Kerilyn said.

"Yeah, you look great," Tracy piped up in agreement.

"They're right. You're pretty stunning yourself," Audra said.

He wore navy slacks, a powder-blue, long-sleeved shirt, and a navy blazer—simple attire that looked amazing on his physique. The diamond earrings sparkled in his ears, and his beard was freshly groomed.

"Thanks. You ready?"

"Almost. I have to pick a purse," Audra said.

"While you do that, I need to check something downstairs. Don't take long. We have reservations."

"I won't," she said.

She went into her closet and, after a few minutes, settled on a gold and black clutch. "All right, girls, let's go."

Kerilyn scooped her little sister off the bed, and the three of them exited the bedroom. They made their way down the stairs, and at the bottom, Junior came racing toward them.

"Daddy said to tell you he'll be right back," he said.

"Where did he go?"

Her son shrugged.

"Well, this is odd, because he told me to hurry and now he's disappeared."

The doorbell rang, and Audra frowned. Who in the world could that be?

To her surprise, Damon stood on the stoop. She flung the door open. "Hon, what are you...?"

Her words faltered when he pulled his hand from behind his back to reveal a bouquet of red roses.

Warmth invaded her chest. "Honey…"

Audra took the flowers and pressed her nose into the petals. The heady fragrance made the night that much more special and reminded her of all the times past he had surprised her with bouquets that brightened her day.

"Thank you," she said softly. "You're the man of my dreams." She cupped the back of his neck and gave him a proper, full kiss.

When he lifted his head, Damon smiled. "You ready?"

"Yes."

Audra placed the flowers on the table in the foyer. "Keri, would you put these in a vase for me?"

"Sure, Mom."

Kerilyn continued to hold Tracy, whose little legs wrapped around her big sister's waist. Junior stood beside them.

"You know that if anything comes up, you can call us," Audra continued.

Her eldest nodded. "And I know to turn on the alarm after you leave."

"Right. And these two should be in bed no later than nine o'clock. If—"

Damon slipped an arm around her waist and pulled her back against him. "Kids, please tell your mom to go so we're not late for dinner."

"Go!" Kerilyn said.

"Go!" the other two echoed, following her lead.

Audra laughed. "Okay, okay. I know you have everything under control." She gave them each a kiss and then took her husband's hand.

"Have fun!" Kerilyn called after them.

Audra returned her attention to the door to see their children waving at them. She waved back.

Damon had taken her white Mercedes out the garage, so she climbed in, and he shut the door. Once settled behind the wheel, he turned on smooth jazz and then reversed down the driveway. He honked the horn, and the kids waved one last time before shutting themselves inside.

"They'll be fine," Damon said.

"I know." She rubbed her hand along his arm, loving the bulky texture of muscles beneath the blazer. "Not tonight, but maybe one date night we can make plans to stay out all night."

"You mean rent a hotel room?" he asked.

"Yes. What do you think?"

"Hell yeah. I like that idea."

Audra giggled at his enthusiasm.

Damon pulled up to the gate, and as they waited for it to open, he said, "Almost forgot. I have one more thing for you." He shifted in the seat. Fishing in his pocket, he pulled out a small bag of jelly beans.

Audra clutched them in her hand as emotion flooded her chest. "You're too much, you know that?" she said in a hoarse voice.

Damon leaned across the console and kissed the corner of her mouth. "That's the way I always want to make you feel," he whispered.

She cupped his jaw and pressed her lips to his, savoring their softness, heart melting at the tenderness and love in his kiss.

When they pulled out of the subdivision, she placed a hand on his thigh, and he covered it with his own. They drove the entire way to the restaurant in that same position, talking softly, laughing, reconnecting.

Audra smiled the entire way, secure in Damon's love, and confident their marriage was back on track.

Bonus Content

If you enjoyed this story, join my mailing list to read a bonus scene with Audra and Damon at their vacation home in the Dominican Republic!

Use the QR code or enter the link below in your browser.

geni.us/DDBonusContent

Also by Delaney Diamond

More from the Family Ties series!

Ethan (Family Ties #1)

After seven years together, one night, Skye broaches the subject of marriage and learns the devastating truth. Ethan has no intention of marrying her.

Monica (Family Ties #2)

Andre is engaged to marry the daughter of the man who gave him a chance when no one else would, but seeing Monica causes old feelings to resurface and calls his plans into question.

Audra (Family Ties #3)

When Audra asks for a divorce, she and Damon are forced to face the truth about their marriage. Can they rekindle the fire in the relationship... before it's too late?

* * *

Read how Sylvie and Oscar reconciled after fifteen years apart in Passion Rekindled.

* * *

Visit my Books page to learn about all my books and the following marriage-in-trouble titles:

Perfect (Johnson Family #2)

For Better or Worse (Hawthorne Family #4)

The Arrangement (Latin Men #1)

Second Chances (Latin Men #5)

* * *

Audiobook samples and free short stories available at
www.delaneydiamond.com.

About the Author

Delaney Diamond is the USA Today Bestselling Author of sensual, passionate romance novels. Originally from the U.S. Virgin Islands, she now lives in Atlanta, Georgia. She reads romance novels, mysteries, thrillers, and a fair amount of nonfiction. When she's not busy reading or writing, she's in the kitchen trying out new recipes, dining at one of her favorite restaurants, or traveling to an interesting locale.

Enjoy free reads on her website. Join her mailing list to get sneak peeks, notices of sale prices, and find out about new releases.

Join her mailing list
www.delaneydiamond.com

facebook.com/DelaneyDiamond
instagram.com/delaneydiamondbooks
twitter.com/DelaneyDiamond
pinterest.com/delaneydiamond